Wolfe's Tales

Wolfe's Tales

Flinders University Creative Writing Student Anthology

Written by
Jack Allen, Mikayla Fox, Rachel Gurr,
William Langrehr, Holly Letcher,
Cara Migalka, Helena Perre,
Elena Sopotsko, and Rose Star

With Editing by
Jack Allen, Rachel Gurr,
William Langreher, Holly Letcher,
Helena Perre, Rose Star,
and Lynette Washington

First published by Glimmer Press 2024
West Beach, South Australia
www.glimmerpress.com.au

A catalogue record for this book is available from the National Library of Australia

ISBN: 978-0-6484635-8-0

Cover images by Abby Guy
Cover design by Abby Guy
Internal images by Abby Guy
Internal design by Lynette Washington

Printed in Australia

The authors and editors of this anthology would like to acknowledge the Kaurna, Ngarrindjeri, and Permanangk peoples, the traditional custodians of the lands on which these stories were conceptualised, written, and published. We acknowledge First Nation peoples' connection to country, cultural heritage, and beliefs. We would like to pay our respects to Elders, past, present, and emerging.

To Lisa, Sean, Amy, and Justina.

Contents

Introduction

When, in 2023, we learned that we would be publishing an anthology of our work, we were incredibly excited. The opportunity to have something tangible come out of our three(-ish) years of study, as well as getting our names out there for the first time, was unexpected but welcome. We are the third group of students to have done this project, which was pioneered by the graduate class of 2021.

Our process of choosing the anthology's theme was comically lengthy, involving polls and an extensive spreadsheet. After hours of class time, we decided on 'antique shop', and many hours (and one scribbly whiteboard) later, we chose to name the owner of said shop 'Wolfe'. To allow our stories to have whatever settings or characters we wanted, we decided that each story would have a unique incarnation of Wolfe who fulfils a different role in each narrative.

Our next struggle, once the stories were written and somewhat workshopped, was choosing our title. Again, discussions, polls, spreadsheets, and messy whiteboards ensued. The struggle we had was how, despite our theme, our stories were vastly different in scope and genre, and encapsulating that in a few words was surprisingly difficult. When, near the end of the workshop, one person spitballed *Wolfe's Tales*, we all had a brief giggle at the pun…and then realised it actually worked quite well.

One thing that made the editing process easier was how many people decided to be involved. Nearly two-thirds of the class were a part of the editorial team, meaning the workload for each person was far more manageable. Based on advice given by some of the 2021 editorial group, we made sure to start out with a structured file system (thanks Jack!), and solid communication networks, which helped immensely with keeping everything on track. We also decided that we wanted the bulk of the editing work done over the summer while we were either on break between semesters, or before starting honours. We divided this time into three rounds of workshopping over about nine weeks, which then left time for some additional editing from our wonderful lecturer and project coordinator, Amy Matthews, before we then sent the manuscript off to Glimmer Press in mid-March.

One of the concepts that we came up with, during workshopping cover ideas, was to give each story an individual image. We had been tossing up using a door on the cover, but decided the concept would work better if each story had a door of its own. We also felt the doors could help indicate setting and tone, as those vary wildly between stories. It also gives the feeling of 'stepping into' the story when you turn that page.

The journey of writing and editing this anthology

has been a bumpy ride, but we're so glad to have done it. We all feel we have learned a lot from the process (even if just the difference in dash types), and we are better writers and editors for it. We're immensely grateful to Flinders University, Amy Matthews, Glimmer Press, and the class of 2021, for paving the way and supporting us during this time.

We also look forward to seeing the work of the groups to come. May your process bring the same learning experiences, and most importantly, as much fun as we all had working on this one!

We sincerely hope that all our hard work shines through, and that you enjoy reading it as much as we enjoyed writing it.

Wolfe's Tales Editorial Team

The Esoteric Charlie Hill

Jack Allen

The courthouse on Queen Alice Road was dark, cold, and foreboding. To the twelve-year-old Charlie Hill, the room was enormous. The vaulted ceiling with its row of grand arches could have crossed the sky itself. The tall, thin windows did not let in much light—despite the day outside being unseasonably clear—and what little was allowed in was faint and lifeless.

Charlie stood alone, staring up at the shadowy figure of the judge who would, in mere minutes, decide his fate. Behind him, seated on the hard-backed benches of the gallery, were some twenty or thirty other children. All were between the ages of seven and twelve and were dressed in the same manner as Charlie: shirts many sizes too big, pants or skirts of a distressingly thin material, and discarded jackets, which were the only real source of warmth they had. The luckier children wore moth-eaten scarfs and flat caps embedded with a thick layer of dirt. They were all silent and waiting in fear for the beast at the end of the

17

hall to wake up.

'Charlie Hill,' boomed the deep voice of the Honourable Judge. The sound cast the room into silence as the soon-to-be defendants held their breaths. 'You stand accused of theft. How do you plead?' Charlie couldn't speak. Helplessly, he stared up to the ferocious, hulking figure of the Honourable Judge Dorian E. Northwich.

'I…' squeaked Charlie. 'I didn't mean to—'

'Guilty or innocent?' the Judge demanded over Charlie's desperate stammer. 'How do you plead? Do not make me ask you again.'

'Well, I did, but I didn't mean to,' Charlie babbled. 'See, Matron wasn't giving us enough food and—'

Bang! Bang! Bang!

'Guilty.' The word bellowed out into the courthouse as if shot from a cannon. It seemed to rattle the windows in their wrought iron frames. Charlie exhaled sharply, all breath lost as if a great blow had struck his gut. He had expected the word; he had no defence nor explanation which could satisfy the Judge. Behind him, in the many rows of the gallery, the waiting children fell further into dread. They all knew that soon enough, the same verdict would come to each of them, and there was no chance of escape.

Once the children had all been tried and found guilty, they were hurried out of the cold courtroom and into a waiting room. After being given a lump of stale bread and a mug of water, the children were told to wait for the potential buyers. They whispered to one another, wondering what futures awaited them.

Lord Marcus Blackwell of Retonshire was the first of the buyers to arrive; he controlled a number of coal mines on his family's once-grand estate. He took only boys, and only those he judged the strongest or most likely to survive. Charlie was not among this selection.

The next buyer was Sister Mary Bennefield, a nun at the nearby convent of Saint June. She took only girls and any she could find; their faith did not matter, as she would correct it in time.

Only a few boys remained, those too scrawny and weak to be of any real use. The next buyer was Mr James Farley, a jeweller of considerable skill and considerably more wealth. He took two boys, those with skilled fingers, keen eyes, and no convictions of thievery.

When the final buyer arrived, only Charlie remained. He was a slightly hunched, portly old man, with a shock of white hair and a great moustache of the same colour. He wore a finely tailored suit with a green velvet jacket, clean leather gloves and a pristine black top hat which he removed upon entering the room.

'Good afternoon, my boy. I am Mr Francis Wolfe, and who may you be?' Wolfe's voice was soft and friendly, unlike anything Charlie had heard that day. It reminded him of a priest who used to visit the Bradford Institute for Orphaned Boys. He would speak with the children and listen to them, a rare occurrence in that uncaring place. Charlie missed him and wondered if he would see the priest again.

'Charlie Hill, sir.' His voice was weak but not frightened; Charlie felt he could trust this man.

'It is nice to meet you, Charlie. Now, to business. I operate a small antique shop with my business partner, Maxwell Griffin. We are looking for someone to work at the shop for us so that we can focus on the restoration of certain items under our care, and the more specialised sales. Firstly, how are your letters? Can you read?'

'A little, sir. Matron made sure we could all read enough to get by.'

'Good. And your numbers? Am I right to assume that your matron ensured your education in that regard as well?'

'Yes, sir. I'm a little slow but I can get it done.'

'Good, but I have a little test to make sure. You sell something for two pounds and five shillings. The customer hands you two guineas and a crown. What change do you give back?'

Charlie thought for a moment before replying.

'Uh, three shillings?' he answered shakily. Wolfe's face broke into a wide smile.

'Very good, my boy. You will do nicely.'

The court's cells, where Charlie had been made to stay until his sale could be finalised, were far from comfortable. But it was not the cold or damp which kept Charlie from sleeping, but his excitement to have escaped the Bradford Institute. As he shivered under a paper-thin blanket each night, Charlie imagined what awaited him in his new life. He pictured finding rings and necklaces of great power, a magic sword which would proclaim him to be the true king. But above the visions of his inevitable heroism, Charlie dreamed of the warm food and comfortable bed Mr Wolfe would give him.

A few days later, Charlie stood outside of number forty-seven Thornton Road, staring up at the intricately painted sign which declared the shop to be Griffin & Wolfe's Esoteric Curiosities. The shop was an old, thin, two-storey building. Bay windows jutted out on either side of the wooden door. The glass was difficult to see through, as a layer of grime distorted the view into the shop. Charlie took a deep breath and adjusted his tattered jacket before he opened the door and stepped inside. A bell tinkled to announce his presence.

The shop was difficult, perhaps impossible, to take in all at once, so densely packed were the shelves and cupboards. They were filled to the brim with an unbelievable variety of objects: hats, books, goblets, and any number of things besides. Charlie found himself dwarfed by both the sagging shelves, and the enormity of the work he would surely find thrust upon him. He worried that Mr Wolfe or Mr Griffin would have him reorganise the store, as it seemed to Charlie that everything was haphazardly placed wherever space could be found.

'Hello? Mr Wolfe? Mr Griffin? It's Charlie,' he

called. He paused as he waited for a response, but none came. He stepped further into the shop and wound his way through the veritable maze of shelves. Charlie eventually found the clerk's desk. It was a small rectangle in the centre of the shop, forming an island mostly free from the numerous antiques. Along with a couple of wooden chests, which Charlie opened to find an impressive collection of books, the desk held a large, ornate metal till. Charlie tapped it experimentally and jumped at the loud ring which signalled the cash drawer opening. He looked around the desk again and found, on an otherwise empty shelf underneath the till, a neatly folded letter addressed to him. Mr Wolfe's handwriting was thin and loopy, so it took Charlie some time to decipher.

Dear Charlie,

My apologies, but I am unable to be at the shop today. I am currently in North Carimshire for my son's wedding. I am unsure when precisely I will be able to return, but it should be within a week. The shop is usually rather quiet; we have a somewhat exclusive clientele.

Should a customer wish to buy an item marked with a red dot, you must tell him he cannot. Those items are for a pre-arranged sale which will be conducted by either Mr Griffin or myself, until I am to teach you how they function.

During your time working here, you will live above the shop. Your room is upstairs at the end of the hall. While I am away, you are expected to open the shop at precisely nine o'clock every morning and will not close until eight o'clock that night. You are of course permitted to take a lunch and dinner break every day, for no longer than an hour, and you should find enough food upstairs to satisfy you until my return.

As I expect you have few appropriate clothes, I have provided you with something more fitting to your job, which you will find in your room upstairs. Since our clientele expect a certain level of professionalism, I have also left you a pocket watch. It is quite old, as it was mine as a boy, and it unfortunately no longer works, but you should find it serviceable enough.

Mr Griffin will be in his office, working on some extremely delicate restorations. I ask that, except in the greatest emergency, you leave him to his work. Please take the rest of the day to acquaint yourself with the shop and the rooms upstairs but be sure to keep an ear out for the bell.

Best wishes,

Mr Francis Wolfe

Charlie reread the letter before he hurried up the narrow staircase, which sagged a little with age. He walked along a hallway past an open door to the kitchen, a locked door with a golden plaque which read '*F. Wolfe*', and a stack of sealed boxes, before he reached the open door to a small bedroom. The room was plainly decorated with a short, empty bookshelf, a wall clock, and low bed as the only furnishings. On the bed was a small pile of clothes. Charlie stood in the doorway for a moment, stunned; the room was significantly nicer than what he had to share at the Bradford Institute. Charlie came to his senses and quickly changed into the clothes Mr Wolfe had provided: a clean white shirt, grey pants, and a green woollen waistcoat into which he put the slightly battered silver pocket watch.

Charlie glanced at the wall clock, its hands declared it to be a quarter past nine. He rushed downstairs to the front door, where he turned over a sign declaring the shop 'open'.

He diligently sat at the clerk's desk for an hour and a half, occasionally flipping through one of the many books, or playing with the till, before he decided that Mr Wolfe's letter was right and he wouldn't be dealing with too many customers.

Charlie decided to finish his tour of the shop. The back half of the store was somehow even more cluttered than the front, with more drawers and counters squeezed into the same space. Along the back wall, Charlie found two rows of shelves lining the path to a black door. The objects on these shelves, all of which appeared to be completely random, and as often as not in a considerable state of disrepair, had been marked with red dots. Beaten up books, weathered top hats, a chipped porcelain teacup, a typewriter, and a feathered quill were all marked the same. While Charlie was looking through the items, he heard a clicking sound, but thought nothing of it. Along the uncovered brick wall was a flat wooden door, which was painted black. It had a round golden doorknob and—a little above Charlie's head—a small, golden plaque which read '*M. Griffin*'. Charlie went to knock and introduce himself to Mr Griffin but remembered Mr Wolfe's letter and lowered his hand.

Having spent much of his life at the Bradford Institute, where food was always scarce and thieves were rarely caught, Charlie had little choice but to sleep lightly. So when, in the early hours of his third day working for Mr Wolfe, there came the creak of a floorboard, Charlie woke instinctively. He lay still, eyes pressed shut and prepared himself to jump out of bed should the need arise. Footsteps grew fainter and seemed to descend the stairs towards the shop floor. Charlie slowly opened his eyes and looked around his small room, which seemed to be as he had left it, apart from the door. It had been closed the night before, but now stood open wide enough to allow a man entrance.

Charlie slid quietly from his bed, another talent learnt at the Bradford Institute, crept along the hallway, past Mr Wolfe's office, and down the stairs. He stopped a little under halfway down and looked out across the shop, trying to find who had been in his room. There was no sign of a light in the shop, and the door and windows seemed in perfect condition, both of which baffled Charlie who was certain he had heard footsteps. Having decided he had imagined the sounds, and that his door had simply not been closed completely, Charlie walked into the kitchen and struck a match from a book he had found the night before. Careful of the flame, he held it up to the face of the grandfather clock which declared the time to be a quarter-past-four. Charlie extinguished the match, returned to his room, and fell quickly asleep, oblivious to the soft thud as a door closed downstairs.

Several hours later Charlie woke to the crackle of bacon and the smell of cooking food. He dressed quickly, left his room, and walked to the kitchen, where he found Mr Wolfe standing over the oven. His jacket hung off the back of a chair and his sleeves were rolled up. He turned around as Charlie entered.

'Good morning, Charlie. I'm glad you found the shop alright. Apologies again for missing your arrival, but it couldn't be helped. How did you sleep? A bit better than in the courthouse cell I would imagine?'

'Yes, sir,' Charlie hesitated, 'but I think someone was in my room last night.'

'Besides you? How peculiar. Could you have heard the building settling? I love this old shop, but she is far from a spring chicken.'

'Maybe…' As Charlie trailed off, Mr Wolfe turned back to the stove. He took a plate and put half of the bacon, a couple of sausages, and an egg on it, then turned back to Charlie.

'Now, my boy, breakfast should really be your job, not mine…'

'Oh. I'm sorry. I didn't realise,' Charlie stammered.

Mr Wolfe's moustache twitched before his face broke into a wide smile and he started chuckling. He passed the plate to Charlie and said, 'Not to worry my boy. I am just playing with you. I am very happy to make breakfast. I do very much enjoy cooking. When my children were your age, I would make a quite wonderful Sunday lunch… But look at me waffling on like the old man I am. Tuck in, Charlie. You must be starving.'

Several hours later, Charlie sat at the clerk's desk and sorted a rather large box of rings by metal and how desperately they required restoration. The bell above the door tinkled. Charlie looked up from the ruby encrusted signet ring he had just picked from the box, and saw a rotund man in a brown suit, the vest of which seemed pushed almost to its limits. The man was taller than Mr Wolfe but not by much, and his set of dark mutton chops made up for the lack of hair on the top of his head. The man walked to the clerk's desk and looked Charlie up and down before his face broke into a wide smile.

'Ah, I see Francis has found some fresh meat,' the man laughed, his deep voice booming across the small shop.

'Yes sir, how can I help you today?' Charlie asked.

'My, he has you well trained. How long have you been here, lad?'

'Just a few days,' Mr Wolfe said, as he walked out from behind a set of shelves. 'Some children come like that.'

'Do they indeed? I wish mine had.'

'Charlie, this is Lord Jonathan Drake.'

'A pleasure to meet you, sir,' Charlie said. He remembered the time Lord Bradford had visited the institute and imagined that Lord Drake would also take unkindly to anything short of complete deference.

'He is one of our more frequent customers. Speaking of,' Mr Wolfe said and turned to Lord Drake, 'I imagine you are here to pick something up?'

'I most certainly am. I've got the blasted ticket

around here somewhere,' he said as he patted himself down. Eventually he pulled a slightly crumpled piece of paper from a waistcoat pocket which he offered to Mr Wolfe.

'To Charlie, if you would not mind. I want to teach him what to do in special cases such as this.'

'Fair enough. Here you go, lad,' he said and handed the paper to Charlie.

'That, Charlie, is a proof of sale. It proves that Mr Griffin or myself have sold something to this gentleman to be picked up at his leisure. If you open it up, it'll say what you need to go get.'

Charlie opened the note which was typed and much easier to read than Mr Wolfe's loopy script.

Proof of Sale — 18/10/1874.

To Lord J. Drake, by Mister M. Griffin.

One copy The Mysteries of Foreman House. *Theodore Moore. 1750. First edition.*

For the sum of ten pounds, three shillings. Paid in full.

'Do you understand it?' Mr Wolfe asked after Charlie looked up from the note.

'Yes, sir.'

'Good. Now, could you go and get it? It will be with the other red dot items, near Mr Griffin's office.'

Charlie nodded his understanding and walked towards the back wall of the shop where he looked over a shelf full of leather-bound books. He soon found Lord Drake's book and pulled it off the shelf. The book fell open in Charlie's hands and as he looked down at it, he spotted his own name. Charlie laughed slightly at the coincidence, closed the book, and walked back to the clerk's desk, where Lord Drake and Mr Wolfe were talking.

'When can I expect the new stock to be ready?' Lord Drake asked.

'I plan to get more use out of it before we sell. Besides we still have plenty available, should you require it,' Mr Wolfe replied rather sternly.

'Sir, your book,' Charlie said, holding it out to Lord Drake.

'Thank you, lad,' he said, and then turned to Mr Wolfe. 'Top of the list, if you don't mind. Good day.'

He nodded to Mr Wolfe, smiled at Charlie, and walked out of the shop, the book held close to his chest like a prize he was afraid to lose.

'That was very well done, Charlie,' Mr Wolfe said.

'Thank you, sir.'

'Can you finish sorting these rings? Then I think we should be clear to close the shop a little early today.'

The next several days passed slowly and without incident. Charlie worked at the clerk's desk, while Mr Wolfe made repairs and periodically left the shop. Today, Mr Wolfe had travelled out of the city to attend an estate sale. When the bell above the door tinkled,

Charlie stood up from the low shelf he was filling with books.

'Hello!' Charlie shouted cheerfully. 'I'll be there in a moment.' He half-jogged back to the clerk's desk and took his place behind it. He was met with the careworn, grime-covered face of a woman. While she was not old, her face was deeply lined, a feature Charlie recognised from the older boys at the Bradford Institute. Her high-collared dress may have been quite fine long before she found it. The navy fabric was stained almost black and had been ripped and repaired countless times. A dark green hat with a stained white flower attached to its brim sat on her grey-streaked hair. It was much nicer than anything else she wore, and Charlie suspected it had been stolen. The woman's eyes had heavy bags and were wet with tears.

'Where is 'e? What 'ave you done to 'im?' The woman cried, her voice cracking.

'I…I don't know what you mean,' Charlie stuttered, taken aback by the woman's tone.

'My son,' she said, as if it should be obvious. 'Walter Rowe? 'e worked 'ere not even two weeks ago and I've not seen or 'eard anything from 'im. What 'ave you done with 'im?'

'I believe I can answer that,' a gravel-voiced man, whom Charlie had not heard enter the shop, said. He was tall, gaunt and dressed like Mr Wolfe in a fine suit except with a dark red velvet jacket and matching silk cravat. Beneath a black bowler hat, his dark hair was slicked back. He looked down at Charlie and nodded, then he wet his lips before he spoke.

'Ah, you must be Charlie. Francis told me about

you. I'm Mr Griffin. It's nice to meet you,' Mr Griffin said, before turning his attention to the weeping Mrs Rowe. 'Now, my dear woman, why don't you come with me to my office? We shall be a little more comfortable there.'

'Alright.' The woman sobbed as she followed Mr Griffin to the back of the shop.

'Oh, Charlie,' he said as he looked back, 'why don't you make a pot of tea to calm Mrs Rowe's nerves?'

'Yes, sir. Right away.'

Charlie rushed upstairs and set about making tea. Before the water began to boil, he heard a cry from downstairs. After a moment's consideration, Charlie decided against investigating the cry, reasoning that if Mr Griffin needed his help, he would call for it. Charlie finished the tea and hurried downstairs to the door of Mr Griffin's office. He knocked as politely as he could but found no response.

'Mr Griffin?' Charlie asked, as he knocked again. 'Is everything okay?' Again, he received no response, so he walked back to the counter to see if Mr Griffin and Mrs Rowe had returned there. Again, Charlie heard the rhythmic clicking which emanated from the red-dotted shelves but thought nothing of it.

Charlie did not hear anything from Mr Griffin for several days. It appeared to him that Mr Griffin had simply vanished. One morning, as he had done for nearly a week, Charlie flipped the sign to 'open' and wandered back to the clerk's desk. There, he found a pristine dark green hat with a spotless white flower in the brim and a red dot pinned to it, beside a letter addressed to him. The script was much easier to read than Mr Wolfe's loopy writing. Mr Griffin's hand was smaller and sharper.

Charlie,

I apologise for not explaining this in person, but I need to meet Francis at the train station. Do not worry about Mrs Rowe. We spoke, and it appeared she was hysterical and had gotten the shops confused. I would have told you this earlier, but my work has been incredibly demanding of late, and I have not found the time.

I recently acquired this hat and have found a buyer. Could you please place it with the other specialty items, until he is able to pick it up.

Yours,

Maxwell Griffin

Charlie didn't quite believe the letter. To him, Mrs Rowe had seemed in her right mind, if rather distressed, but he was convinced that Mr Griffin knew best. Charlie picked up the hat and carried it to the two shelves of marked items.

As he stood in front of a shelf and tried to decide where would be best to put the hat, he noticed the repetitive clicking. He looked around, confused, and saw a typewriter with a red dot covering half of the manufacturer's name. The peculiar thing was that the keys were moving on their own.

Charlie put the hat down in the first place he could find, crossed to the typewriter, and watched its keys move downwards one by one.

'L-P—H-E-L-P—H-E-L-P—H'

'What?' As Charlie spoke the keys froze for a moment before they began to click down again, faster than before. Charlie followed the movement of the keys so carefully that he failed to hear a soft tinkle coming from the front of the shop.

'C-A-N—Y-O-U—H-E-A-R—M-E'

'I think so. What are you?'

'I—A-M—W-A-L-T-E-R—R-O-W-E—Y-O-U—H-A-V-E—T-O—H-E-L-P—U-S'

'Walter Rowe? That woman was looking for you.'

Slowly Walter typed, 'M-O-T-H-E-R'

'What happened to you?'

'G-R-I-F-F-I-N—T-R-A-P-P-E-D—U-S'

'Trapped you? Why?'

'Well, Charlie,' sneered Mr Griffin as he walked towards the typewriter, Mr Wolfe at his side, 'it is because, like you, Walter, and poor Mrs Rowe, got nosy and started looking into that which did not concern them.' He slammed the lid of the typewriter's box down, muffling Walter's furious clicking.

'Looking into what? I don't know what's happening!' Charlie squeaked.

'I know, my boy,' Mr Wolfe sighed sadly, 'but I am afraid you now know something is happening, and my associate here does not care for loose ends.'

'You might as well tell him. He won't talk to anyone else,' Mr Griffin growled.

'Very well. As I said, Mr Griffin here is my business partner, and he has friends in very powerful, if non-conventional, places. Some years ago, he approached me and offered to bring prosperity to me and my family in exchange for a small cost.' Mr Wolfe's voice was still soft and seemed almost to pity Charlie. 'Only a few people a year, those nobody would care about if they went missing. Mr Griffin holds these people here until he, or his kin, needs them for…'

'Sustenance,' Mr Griffin supplied. He grinned, revealing sharp fangs.

'Indeed.' Mr Wolfe grimaced. 'That is all you need to know. Oh Charlie, I am sorry. You did have potential.' He turned his back and walked away. 'Mr Griffin, do what you must.'

Mr Griffin slowly approached Charlie, ignoring his screams.

Many days passed, or perhaps it was weeks or years— Charlie had lost count. He sat stiffly on a shelf beside a weathered top hat, a feather quill and a typewriter with a dark hole where its keys had once been. Through the clock face of his gifted, slightly battered, silver pocket watch, he looked out into the store and watched a young girl with ragged clothes and unbrushed hair enter the shop and find the letter under the till from Mr Wolfe.

Ronnie and the Amulet of Adventure

Helena Perre

Ronnie's legs pedal faster than ever before.

Really, it's not her fault she has to speed to The Hill. Why did her mum take a whole twenty minutes to tell her that Wolfe's is back in town? If she'd woken her up as soon as she'd found out, Ronnie wouldn't be worried about getting there too late.

Now she stands on the pedals because it makes her go faster and feel taller, and she needs all the help she can get. The air whips against her face. Her heart is pumping so fast she can hear it in her ears. It's the feeling she's been waiting for all year, the anticipation, the thrill of *adventure*.

Riding next to Ronnie, not nearly as enthusiastic, are her two best friends, Van and Charles. All around them are kids, mostly younger, speeding on their bikes.

Some cars head in the same direction, driven by the tired-looking parents of excited young children, and those few lucky enough to have flying abilities travel through the air.

'Woah!' Ronnie shouts, as hard bubbles form under the grass to create mini hills. She swerves to avoid a bump, narrowly missing Van and Charles. She whips her head around to find a group of sixth-graders she recognises from school snickering as they race behind the trio. One of them flicks his wrist and another bump in the ground almost knocks Ronnie over.

Damn earth mages.

'Charles, take them out!' Ronnie yells, right as the group starts gaining on them. 'Or push them back.'

'No! That's—ah!' Charles gets cut off by a bump in the ground.

'Just use your air powers to give us a boost!' Ronnie yells over the wind.

'It's unethical!' Charles declares.

Ronnie pushes harder on her pedals. She takes the lead, speeding through the town square where more townsfolk abandon their activities to join the race to Wolfe's. Ronnie cuts through town alongside the grotto where the naiads and merfolk gossip.

The Hill is in sight now, and so is the store, in all its glory. The deceivingly small yellow hut with a faded sign on its roof sits on the highest point of The Hill, as it does every summer. Ronnie jumps off her bike, deserting it at the bottom of the incline. Clambering uphill, using her hands to propel her faster on the particularly steep part, she finally reaches the top.

Ronnie pants and leans over with her hands on her knees, trying to catch her breath.

'Merlin and Morgana,' Van says, frustrated. 'Chill at all?'

Ronnie scrunches her eyebrows. 'Boring at all? It's Wolfe's!' Her voice turns wistful, as she spins to face the store. 'Finally! Time for magic, for *adventure!*' There's a sparkle in her eyes. 'Right, Charles?'

Charles heaves himself to the top of The Hill, puffing for air. 'Sure,' he wheezes.

An asthmatic boy with air powers. Ronnie laughs to herself.

'But it is like, more for kids,' he says as he pulls out a puffer from his pocket.

Kids. The word lingers in Ronnie's head, the way he said it, like it doesn't apply to them anymore. Like it's a distant, faraway word.

The people they're racing against rush past them, straight into the store, pulling Ronnie back to reality.

'No!' Ronnie says, pulling his arm back up. 'We gotta go nooow! Get the good stuff before it goes,' she pleads.

Van rolls her eyes. 'It'll be fine.'

'Apparently,' Charles starts slowly, still trying to get enough air into his lungs, 'there are more storeys this year.'

Ronnie's brows rise and she gives a low whistle. 'Wolfe has got to be some kind of matter mage.

There's no way so much can fit in that tiny place.'

'Of course it can. It's literally magic,' Van counters. 'The whole town is magic.' She cringes.

Ronnie's eyes flick down, and the prickles of embarrassment begin to form under her skin. *Head down and get by,* as her grandparents would always say.

'Sorry, I didn't mean—'

'Let's just go,' Ronnie interrupts. She didn't need to be reminded that she was different than, *less* than, everyone else, just like her grandparents. They were Mazinian, a race as non-magical as it was small. They had never taught Ronnie, nor her mother, of their culture, of their homeland—they just wanted to fall in with the rest of the town. Except Ronnie feels like she sticks out like an un-magic sore thumb.

Ronnie yanks Charles up and drags him towards the entrance, desperate to find something that could finally make her blend in.

Walking inside the store washes all her frustration away.

Charles is right, it's at least four storeys high, with winding staircases and ladders leading to who-knows-what. Old artefacts and magical relics—like the bones of (supposedly) ancient wizards—cover the light yellow walls and fill the cases. Dark wooden shelves hold books, some in languages Ronnie doesn't recognise, and objects. Swords, jewels, talismans, even a magical belt buckle, decorate the shop. It's like looking at a jumble of puzzle pieces before they're put together to make the whole picture. At the back of the ground floor is a clerk's desk, behind which Wolfe sits.

Slight wrinkles run across their tanned skin, their black hair starting to grey. There is a warmth to their smile as they overlook all the customers, a cosiness that matches the store itself. It still has the same aura of magic; the air changes the second you walk over the threshold, and you're bewitched.

Despite being taller than eighty percent of the clientele, the trio can still barely move without being crushed. Children's arms flail about—their guardians exhausted—elbows poke into their ribs, and the screams of excited kids pierce Ronnie's eardrums as she tries to traverse the store.

'Ow,' Van shrieks, after a trollish child steps on her toe. 'Ugh, that's enough.' She clears her throat and holds her head high.

'She's doing the *thing*,' Charles whispers to Ronnie, eyes instantly laced with anxiety.

'Nice to see someone can use their powers for good,' Ronnie teases back. His brows only furrow further.

Van opens her mouth, and it's like Ronnie can see it in slow motion. People's heads turn, their eyes gloss over, and they are entranced by the voice of the siren.

'*Excuse me.*' Van's statement is firm and direct, but it comes out like a gentle caress, like she's trying to woo the store patrons.

The crowd parts, letting the trio pass through, Van leading the way like royalty. Van has siren ancestry, though you wouldn't know just from looking—she doesn't have a fish tail or gills—but you can hear it when she sings and hits notes that shouldn't be possible. It's obvious in the way that anyone who comes across her is drawn to her, and everyone she walks past does a double take. It's things like this that make Ronnie jealous of Van. Not that she wants to entrance everyone, she just wants something *interesting* to happen to her.

When they make their way across the floor to the staircase, Van releases her hold on the patrons. They all return to normal, the kids barely noticing, but Ronnie sees in the eyes of the adults that it was a risky move. Van's lucky she's still too young to get in too much trouble.

They make their way up one of the spiral staircases to the second level, which is still crowded, but at least navigable. Ronnie sees a group of dryads examining a collection of terrariums, all featuring flora from another realm, and next to them, a truth revealing mirror; what Ronnie would give to see a shapeshifter in front of *that*. Van heads to the vintage-style jewellery, while Charles shoots for the ancient rune books. Normally Ronnie would follow him towards the books, but not today. Not in Wolfe's. Not where she can find adventure that isn't in a book. She wanders around for a while, looking for something spectacular. She considers, then disregards, a miniature wishing well, a pair of golden dice, and an antique hairbrush.

Finally, something grabs her eye, and she can't bring herself to ignore it.

'This is the one.' Ronnie nods, certain.

A golden chain dangles from a nail in the wall. The large pendant is a purple gemstone encased in a thick rim of gold. Engraved on the border, which is slightly tarnished yet still glistening, are ancient runes. Ones that Ronnie doesn't recognise.

Charles' eyes widen. 'Woah, what do you reckon it is?'

Ronnie speaks like she's in a trance. 'I don't know, but it's gotta be, like, exploding at the seams with magic. Look at it.' Everything about it seems to glisten, even its tarnish. It calls to Ronnie, begging her to figure it out.

'Maybe it's a wizard's amulet. Or a pirate relic?' he supplies.

Van seems less enthusiastic. 'It could just be a pretty necklace…'

'No, it can't be.' She takes it off the wall, determined to stay afloat. She starts to march down the stairs to the clerk's desk. 'This will be our adventure. We just have to figure out what it does.'

Ronnie's first idea is to leave it in moonlight overnight.

'It could be part of the lunar genus,' she poses to her friends. Who, again, aren't as enthused as they should be.

So, Ronnie sets it in the centre of her backyard, right where the moon's rays can hit it.

The next morning, she rushes outside, still in her pyjamas, hair unbrushed, feet bare, to check on it.

'Morning, honey,' her mum says over her coffee.

Ronnie speeds past her and barely manages a 'G'morning' before she's out the door. The necklace is in the same spot she left it, resting on the grass. She picks it up for inspection. Everything looks the same, though Ronnie swears that the gemstone is shinier than it had been. She looks around the yard, as if something could have appeared overnight. Nothing.

'Whatcha got there?' her mum asks. 'Looks pretty.'.

Ronnie shrugs. 'It's nothing.' She pockets the necklace, but not before her mum gets a quick glance at it. Her eyebrows furrow.

'Is tha—'

'Are you working today?' Ronnie quickly intervenes. The last thing she wants is her mum meddling her way into her adventure and finding out *why* she needs one. She can't just say that she yearns for something magic in her blood. It's not that she's ashamed of her heritage, more that she doesn't feel like she has any heritage to be proud of.

Ronnie's mum shakes the strange look off her face.

'I've got the day off today,' she says as she stirs her coffee. 'Want to go to the beach? Or see a movie?'

Ronnie freezes. 'Maybe another time? I already have plans today. Sorry.'

She isn't sorry, though. Not really.

Her mum doesn't say anything for a second, and Ronnie can see the gears turning.

'That's okay, honey.' The words come out with a forced pleasantness. 'We've got all summer.' A smile plasters over her face. Ronnie internally winces. She *doesn't* have all summer.

'Of course, maybe next week.'

Head down and get by.

The day after that, Van suggests they go to the grotto.

'Oh, great idea! Maybe it activates with water. I wonder if salt and freshwater could make a difference—or maybe the merfolk know something…' Ronnie feels like she's solving an equation with a missing variable. Impossible. At least at her middle-school level.

'Oh, right…I meant we should go for a swim, but we'll definitely try that, too.' The tension in her words latches onto Ronnie's brain. She tries to shake it off, but its claws stay there, tight. Ronnie's jaw sets in annoyance.

Charles looks between them, anxious. 'Yeah, I'm sorry my rune books didn't give any info on its markings, Ron.'

'It's okay. I appreciate the effort.'

They venture down to the grotto, and Van sets up her towel on the top level of the rocks. Charles follows suit and pulls out a book to start reading. Ronnie sits upright, observing the scene around her. Teens muck around on the rocks, cannonballing into the ocean. Some water mages have a long-distance water fight down in the shallows. Ronnie watches them, knowing she and her friends will be there soon—grown up and effortlessly cool. Free of the purgatory that is middle school, where childhood innocence dies, and acne is born.

'It's so hot.' Van fans herself with her hands.

Charles waves his hand softly. 'I got you.' A cool breeze passes over them.

'Thanks,' she replies. Van is already like those kids, Ronnie thinks. She watches Van as she comfortably soaks in the sun, her dark skin glistening like it is enchanted. Van has an ease to her existence that Ronnie hasn't yet mastered. She figures that *trying* to master it defeats the purpose, though.

Ronnie stays sitting up, watching the ocean for a mermaid to pop her head above water. Eventually, she sees a purple tail break through the surface.

'Finally!' She jumps up, with more eagerness than she's had all day. 'Guys, coming?'

'I think I'd rather just relax,' Van replies dryly.

'Same,' Charles says, though Ronnie can tell there are nerves in his words.

'Fine,' she huffs. She treks down the rocks alone.

'Hello!' Ronnie shouts once she's close enough to where the mermaid floats. She's purplish with long, seaweed-textured hair. Ronnie is surprised to see that she doesn't share the same eyes as Van and her family, who all have an alluring greyish colour, like that of a sea storm. The eyes of the mermaid are soothing and trustworthy.

Now that she is face-to-face with one, Ronnie becomes awfully aware that she's never spoken to a mermaid before. Do they have a customary greeting? Or tricky riddles to answer?

Apparently, they speak a different language.

The mermaid's webbed hands move and dance around each other in a form of sign language Ronnie hasn't seen before.

Panicked, she yells out, 'Van! Come help translate!' Heads of other beach-goers turn in confusion, and Ronnie knows that Van is probably dying of embarrassment, but she figures this is more important. 'Please!' she hastily tacks on.

Van begrudgingly makes her way down to Ronnie and the mermaid. Van glares at Ronnie but begins to move her hands with much less precision and confidence than the mermaid. Ronnie figures it's decent enough because the mermaid signs back. Van then points to the necklace, which hangs around Ronnie's neck.

The mermaid shakes her head. Ronnie's heart sinks.

'Ask if putting it in water will activate anything.'

Van signs and gestures to the water. Again, the mermaid shakes her head and Ronnie's heart sinks with it.

The two turn away, Ronnie's head low and Van's voice pierced with annoyance. 'Told you it wouldn't work.'

Three days later, the trio sits in a circle in Ronnie's

lounge room. The necklace sits in the middle on top of an old cushion, its purple gem glaring at Ronnie.

'So, we've tried the moon and the water.' Ronnie ticks each item off with a finger. 'We asked the fire *and* earth ambassadors if it belongs to their heritage, went to the Librarians—'

Charles shudders. 'Never again.'

'Agreed,' Van nods.

Ronnie ignores them, '*And* we went back to Wolfe's to ask about it and got nothing.' She gives a loud groan and flops on the carpet, covering her face with her arms. 'This sucks.'

'It's okay.' Van's too-casual voice says. Ronnie stays down, releasing a deep sigh.

'No, it's not.'

Ronnie can practically hear Van's jaw set.

'Why not?' Her voice toes the line of frustration.

'Because!' *How will they understand?*

'Guys…' Charles starts, anxiety creeping all over his face. They ignore him.

'Because you're too obsessed with everything,' Van snaps.

'Van, don't.' Charles' panic goes unnoticed again.

'No, I'm not—'

'Yes, you are,' Van bites back. 'Nothing can just *be* with you. It has to be bigger, or more epic or more adventurous.'

'So what?' Ronnie crosses her arms childishly.

'What's wrong with wanting to have fun?'

'Nothing, but it's not about having fun with you. It's about nothing ever being enough. Why can't this stupid necklace be enough as it is, why can't *we*?'

'You guys don't get it. You have magic built inside you. I don't have anything.'

'You don't need to have *anything*,' Charles tries, his voice small. 'You have us, that's all we need.'

'*We're* meant to be your adventure. Us riding our bikes in a race against town is an adventure. Talking to mermaids is an adventure. Hanging out in your backyard eating ice blocks can be an adventure. Why can't you just *stop and listen*.' The last part comes out strong and powerful, with her siren's voice.

Ronnie steps back. Van clasps her hand over her mouth with her eyes wide.

Ronnie does stop, not because it works, but because she's too stunned to try again. *Did she really just do that?*

No, she didn't.

Van's face is red and her eyes filled with fear. She didn't do it on purpose. 'I-I'm so sorry,' she splutters out between big breaths. It's the first time Ronnie's ever seen her like this. 'It was an accident—'

'Hey, kiddos,' Ronnie's mum's voice breaks through the house.

Van looks close to tears, anger washed away by her panic and shock. Ronnie's head is swarming with everything but logic, and Charles is looking between them, unsure how to proceed.

'Uh, hi,' he eventually gets out.

Ronnie's mum sees the scene in front of her, and furrows her brows. 'What's going on?'

'Nothing.' Ronnie finally says, her mother's words seeming to snap her back to reality. Her mum surveys the three kids; their faces scarlet from embarrassment.

'Ron, what's wrong?'

Ronnie can't bring herself to answer; she doesn't know what to say.

'Ronnie's necklace doesn't work.' Van manages, her voice creaky.

'What, the chain is broken?'

'No, like it's not doing magic. And apparently, according to Ronnie, that means it's broken.'

Ronnie is stuck, half wanting to hide her face in shame, half wanting to bite back, but not knowing what to say without sounding petulant. She needs to get out, away from everyone's eyes and their minds.

She lets out a mangled huff and ignores the tears that begin to sting her eyes as she storms up the stairs to her bedroom.

After some time—minutes, hours, days, Ronnie isn't sure—there's a knock on the door.

'No,' Ronnie says, muffled.

The door creaks open, and her mum walks in. She delicately sits on the bed.

'Hi, honey.'

'Go away,' Ronnie's faint but petulant voice

responds.

'I have to tell you something first.'

For a second, Ronnie imagines her mother telling her they are actually descendants of some long-lost society of people, and Ronnie is the only one who can save the world or something.

'Your necklace isn't magic—'

'I know. You don't have to rub it in.'

Her mum marches on, ignoring Ronnie's interruption. 'It's a Mazinian coming-of-age chain.'

Ronnie's head shoots out from under the covers.

'What? How do you know that?'

'I recognised the words around it,' she says, nonchalant. 'They're not ancient runes, they're Mazinian.'

Ronnie's eyebrows raise at this.

'Our language,' her mum finishes hesitantly, like she's testing out the words.

'What do they say?' Ronnie's voice is quiet.

'It says "my light".' Her fingers trace the symbols as she reads them.

'Oh.' The news shakes Ronnie, and she doesn't know how to feel. Shocked? Excited? 'Cool.' Her voice is lost.

'You're disappointed.'

'No…yes…'

'That's okay. Reality doesn't always meet

expectations…that doesn't mean it can't hold a specialness though.' Her mum strokes Ronnie's head. 'These necklaces, they're ancient tokens of maturity. Young children would have them gifted when they came of age, probably around your age now. Maybe a bit older. It was to symbolise that this person,' she points her finger at Ronnie's heart, 'was just as important and big as the adults. It may not be magic, but it still tells a story.'

'It has its own adventure,' Ronnie says, voice still husky.

'Exactly.' Her mum smiles.

'How do you know this stuff? Grandma and Grandpa wouldn't have told you.'

'No, they didn't. I found out for myself. I'm sorry I never shared it with you…I guess I was scared that they were right, and that hiding who we are was the safest thing to do for you.' There's a mix of sorrow and hope in her eyes that Ronnie can't decipher.

Ronnie reaches out for her mum's hand, a small smile forming. 'I don't want to be scared of those things.'

'I'm glad. I'm sorry for making that choice for you.' She hesitates before continuing. 'If you would like, we could learn Mazinian history together, learn about our world. I'd love to relearn it alongside you.'

Ronnie's smile comes full force now, and she takes the necklace from her mother's hands. She places it around her neck.

'That sounds great. Just promise you won't make me read a textbook during summer,' Ronnie giggles out the last part.

'Deal.' Her mum holds out her hand.

Ronnie takes it and shakes.

Ronnie heads down the stairs, wrapped in her bedding like a protective shield that will save her from the embarrassment of having to face her friends.

She feels for the necklace around her neck and its cool touch gives her a boost of confidence.

Ronnie heads to the living room, except Van isn't there. Her stomach drops when she sees Charles sitting alone on the floor. He lifts his head up at the sound of her padding.

'It's not too late,' he says, reading her mind. 'She just went home, wanted to give you space. Figured I should stay here to tell you so you wouldn't freak out.'

Her heart regains some balance.

'That's good,' she says, nervous. 'Did I totally screw up?'

'No,' he says, not a trace of doubt in his voice. 'You did a little bit, though. But so did she.' He's so certain, no longer standing for any tension. 'So, you're gonna go talk to her and sort this out?'

'Come with me?'

'Of course.'

The two friends ride their bikes to Van's house, and after being greeted by Van's slightly scary older sister, Ronnie and Charles are in Van's backyard. Van lies in the grass by the pool. She's curled in the foetal position, her shoulders tightly slumped into her chest, her toes curled like she's in pain, and her eyes squeezed shut. Charles takes a spot next to Van. Ronnie stays standing.

Ronnie clears her throat, unsure what the best course of action is. 'Hey,' she starts, and Van's eyes burst open.

'Hi.' She scrambles upright, bits of grass stuck in her hair. 'I'm sorry.' Her face is still frazzled and panicked, but the sight of her two friends seems to ground her ever so slightly.

'Are you okay?' Ronnie asks.

Van shrugs, like a scared little kid. 'Are you?'

Ronnie also shrugs, but in a nonchalant, *whatever* type of way. 'Yeah, but I have some apologising to do. So I won't be good until we are. I'm sorry for being a bad friend. Not appreciating the right things.' She turns to Charles too, who gives her an understanding smile in return.

'Forgiven,' he says, and turns to Van who simply hides her head.

'I'm sorry, too.' Her voice is quiet, like she's scared to speak again and Ronnie realises that she literally is scared of her voice.

'Hey, it's okay. I know it wasn't on purpose.' This doesn't seem to ease her.

'But it still worked! That's horrible! I never want to control you guys.' Her words are wracked with guilt.

Ronnie furrows her brows. 'It didn't work.'

Van's head shoots up. 'What? But you stopped?'

'Yeah, because I was shocked. Dude, you could never do that to us. We actually love you—it wouldn't work.'

'I can confirm this. Says so in the *Mythical Oceans* guide. A siren's voice only works on people who don't care for one another,' says Charles.

'Oh…' Van says, tossing the new information around in her head. 'That's good. That's really good.' Her voice picks up.

'So, your unnecessary apology is accepted,' Ronnie says.

'Thanks. So is yours.'

'Thank the High Mages,' Charles exhales, 'I don't know if I could've handled being a child of divorce this summer.'

Van pauses, considering her next words. 'You know, we love you no matter how you are, and we want *you* to love you no matter how you are.'

Ronnie nods in agreement.

Van lets out a dry chuckle and gestures to herself. 'Look at me, a siren who can't control her own powers—my powers are literally about control!'

'And I'm an asthmatic air mage!' Charles chips in, laughing. 'No one's perfect.'

The girls laugh at him, Van ruffling his hair while Ronnie sits down in the grass next to her. She opens her arms wide and encases them both in a hug, squeezing them tight. They squeeze back.

'Nice necklace,' Van says, after they let go. Ronnie smiles, but still blushes slightly.

'Thanks.' She puffs out her chest, lungs filling with pride.

'It suits you.'

'Yeah, it'll look great when we go on our adventures.'

The setting sun illuminates them and turns the whole backyard into a vibrant blaze of orange. The usually dusty red bricks are a bright terracotta, and the sky is the blue that only exists in dreams and summer. Van's skin is glistening, and Charles' hair is shining a light chestnut under the sun's rays. Ronnie smiles, truly content and at peace.

It's all magic.

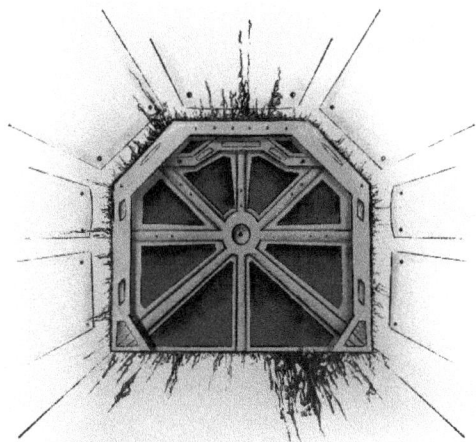

Matter

Mikayla Fox

Planet Mors – Year 2824

'Careful with that, it's incredibly delicate,' the doctor warned.

A gloved hand grasped the small glass vial. It was filled with a glittering black matter that wove in and around itself. It was comprised of molecules with a sharp exterior, almost like miniscule shards of obsidian.

A man in a long black coat with silver hair approached the soldier. He spoke with a gravelly murmur, 'Hand it here. That is not a toy.'

'Yes sir.'

The doctor rose from his chair, nervousness clear in his voice. 'This is to be handled with the utmost care during transportation. If you are exposed, there will be global…perhaps universal consequences—'

The man in the black coat spoke irritably, 'Yes, yes,

Doctor. We're perfectly aware by now. End of the world and all that. Your release will be processed before the suns have set.'

The doctor shook his head. 'This is a mistake.'

The man studied the vial with greedy eyes. 'We'll see.'

City of Commercium – Year 2826

Lorna breathed a sigh of relief, admiring the neon lights that shone brightly against the darkness of space as the SS *Malum* approached the floating city. Ships from all corners of the cosmos made their way towards the docks, hoping to make their fortune. Or to find a decent drink and cause some trouble.

'What a shithole,' Archer said, matter-of-factly.

Jacobi smiled from where she sat, huddled behind a monitor displaying various maps and codes. 'You think every city is a shithole, Archer. If it were up to you, you'd have enough credits to buy your own planet just so you'd never have to speak to another human being.'

'I speak to you lot, don't I?'

Lorna shook her head, amused by Archer's defence.

'Ah yes, the sacrifices we make to survive. Tragic,' Jacobi taunted.

'Piss off, Jacobi. Just stick to your job and fly this hunk of metal,' Archer said, hiding a smile.

'Well, if it's just "a hunk of metal" then why do you

work so hard at keeping it running perfectly?'

Archer was the best engineer in council space—which was the exact reason Lorna had recruited him, despite his attitude. And while the SS *Malum* was a dull, grey ship that lacked the lavish colours and artifacts of a richer crew, it was a home away from home.

Lorna turned in her chair, speaking from the centre of the ship's bridge, 'Alright, children, play nice. We've got some credits to make.'

'Yes, Captain Lorna.' Jacobi began the landing procedure.

'You got it, Cap. Hop-to, Jacobi. I need a drink.' Archer sauntered from the bridge, making his way towards the hanger.

The crew wove through the busy streets of Commercium. The city was full of colour, and most visitors who didn't have to live there considered it beautiful. It was a comforting sight after a long voyage through the cold darkness of space and failed expeditions to dead planets. It offered somewhere to have a hot meal, lay your head and, if you were lucky, make a small fortune. Though, for those who called it home, Commercium proved a rough place to make a living. Many of its inhabitants were poor and living on the streets. Only the traders thrived in cities like this. There were very few houses in Commercium; it was mostly just a floating clutch of businesses selling all kinds of wares. Ward's Weapons for Hire, Fielders & Co Spacecrafts, Exotic Species from the Outer Rims, and of course, Wolfe's Intergalactic Antiquities.

Maverick Wolfe was perhaps the most successful businessperson in the entire sector. No one could quite understand why. His shop was certainly filled with beautiful things, but not beautiful enough to be credited for the vast fortune he boasted. It was said by those who inhabited the streets outside his shop that there were regular visits from shady-looking individuals during the less active hours of the city's constant night. Who exactly they were was anyone's guess. That's the way Lorna preferred it—she didn't need anyone poking their noses into her business.

A harsh ring sounded as they entered the brightly lit shop. It appeared much smaller from the outside and gave the impression that you'd stepped into another world entirely. The shelves were crammed with strange artefacts and things that looked like space junk.

'You're late,' an impatient voice echoed, weaving its way around the shelves to reach the crew.

'The docks were busier than usual today, Wolfe. What do you expect us to do about that?' Archer replied.

A man appeared from behind one of the shelves. He held a walking stick of silver and sapphire and sported a lavish maroon coat that reached his ankles.

'I was not speaking to you, Mr Archer. Your crew is becoming unruly, Captain.'

'Might need to invest in some hair dye there, Maverick. I'm spotting some greys,' Archer teased. Maverick appeared highly unimpressed.

Lorna stepped forward. 'My apologies for Archer, Maverick. Our lateness was out of my control,' she said, giving Archer a pointed look.

'Well, let's not waste another moment. This job happens to be rather time sensitive.'

'How so?' Lorna questioned.

Maverick glanced from Lorna to Archer and Jacobi. 'I would prefer to discuss the details of this job with you in private. You may fill your crew in later, as you see fit.'

'Jacobi,' Lorna said, 'take Archer to the tavern for a drink, won't you?'

'Yes, Captain.' She watched as Jacobi grabbed an irritated Archer by the arm and dragged him from the shop.

'Alright, Maverick, lay it out for me.'

'This is not your regular job, Captain Lorna. You will not be going to rummage through space junk.'

'So, what is it that we're retrieving for you this time?'

'A highly delicate and extremely valuable item. That is all you need to know.'

Lorna was not pleased. 'That's not enough.'

Maverick hesitated for a moment. 'Walk with me.'

He made his way to a living area. Maverick retrieved a metal poker from its stand and fiddled with the fire, watching the flames dance.

'Come on,' Lorna urged. 'Time is money.'

'As you wish. It is a weapon that was created in a lab operating on the planet Mors.'

Lorna scoffed and lowered herself into an

armchair beside a shelf filled with preserved organics. 'There is nothing on Mors…it's a dead planet.'

'Incorrect,' Maverick retorted. 'The weapon was taken from Mors by a high-security spacecraft, military-grade. But the military has denied any involvement. Shortly after leaving the planet, all contact with the crew was lost. This was two years ago and the location of the weapon is currently unknown.'

Lorna sighed, touching her fingers to her forehead. 'Then how do you expect us to find it?'

'I received an anonymous tip as to the ship's whereabouts. But this will not be an easy "in-and-out" retrieval. As I said, the ship is military-grade, and the personnel onboard are likely armed and highly trained.'

'And why the hell would I put myself and my team in a situation like that? This is not what we do, and you know it. Why us?'

'I need a crew that I can trust.'

Lorna snorted. 'Don't bullshit me. You don't trust anyone, Maverick.'

'I need a crew who I've worked with before and I know can get the job done,' Maverick conceded.

'What's in it for us?'

'A hundred-thousand credits—when the job is done.'

Lorna's breath hitched momentarily, but she quickly returned to looking casually interested.

'I'm not a fool, Maverick. I want half up-front.'

He considered this for a moment, and finally, with a decidedly irritated demeanour, Maverick Wolfe stuck out his hand. Lorna grasped it and gave it one firm shake.

'Pleasure doing business with you.' She smiled victoriously. They had been struggling for so long, picking at scraps for what felt like spare change. Lorna was finally able to envisage a real future. One where she and her crew could pursue lives of their own choosing, and not out of necessity and desperation.

Lorna watched as Archer's eyes went so wide they almost fell out of his head. 'A hundred-thousand credits! Holy fu—'

'Archer, get your shit together,' Jacobi spat as she shoved him hard in the shoulder.

It had been two hours since the crew had left Commercium, and Lorna had only just revealed the vague details of the new job.

Jacobi looked to her expectantly. 'So, where are we heading?'

'To riches!' Archer cheered.

'Can it, Archer!' Jacobi threw a sealed packet of crappy space food directly at Archer's face. He caught it and flashed a smug smile.

'Enough, the both of you,' Lorna scolded, turning to hide her amusement.

'Sorry, Cap,' Jacobi and Archer said in unison.

'The tip Maverick received told him that the ship is located somewhere in the twelfth sector.'

Archer's jaw dropped. 'What? No way!'

'Cap, this has to be one of the incredibly rare times where I agree with Archer. We can't go to the twelfth sector. The Council banned travel anywhere near it.'

Lorna looked at Jacobi with a raised eyebrow. 'Yes, Jacobi…because we always abide by the law of the Council.'

Silence.

Lorna sighed. 'Listen, I know this is risky, but think about what these credits could do for us. I could buy a new ship and operate legitimately. There would be no more scavenging for space junk. Jacobi, you could afford to attend the academy. You could become a pilot for the military. This isn't the life I would've chosen for myself and it's not the life my family wanted for me. I know this isn't where you both wanted to end up either.' She hesitated a moment before turning to Archer, 'How long has it been since you saw your little girl?'

He looked down. 'Too long. I told her I'd come back when I could give her a better life.'

Lorna nodded. 'This is how we do that. But I need to know you're both with me.'

She paced the cabin, waiting for their answer. Archer and Jacobi shared a look and turned to Lorna.

'We're with you,' Jacobi said.

'Every step of the way, Cap,' Archer agreed.

Lorna smiled.

'Okay,' Lorna continued, 'this is going to be dangerous. We're dealing with military-grade shit here. And no one, not even Maverick, knows what this weapon is. The only thing he could tell me about it is that it is under no circumstances to come into physical contact with any of us.'

'Why not?' Jacobi questioned.

'I don't know…but he was very adamant about it, and I know better than to discard a warning from Maverick.'

'Alright. Well, let's get this shit done then. We've got credits to make,' Archer said, opening the packet of food and downing it in one go.

Jacobi rolled her eyes. 'Of course that's all you have to say about this whole thing.'

Archer only shrugged. 'I've got my priorities straight.'

Jacobi scanned her monitor. 'Captain, we're thirty minutes out of the twelfth sector. How do you want to proceed?'

'Turn off all unnecessary power. Especially the lights. Anything that could be detected by potential security measures has to go. We don't know what the Council is trying to hide out here, but we can assume they've taken heavy precautions to keep it out of the public's knowledge.'

Jacobi nodded. 'Copy that. Going dark.'

'Light's out, fuckers,' Archer said dramatically.

Jacobi rolled her eyes as Archer gave her a wink.

The SS *Malum* coasted gently across the boundary of the twelfth sector. It was silent, like space always was. No alarms, no military ships…*nothing*.

'I thought there'd be some kind of ruined city or dead planet, or something.' Jacobi looked at the scanners, confused. 'I'm not picking anything up.'

'Keep looking. There must be something here. There's fifty-thousand credits riding on it,' Lorna urged, pacing once again.

They continued in silence for another hour. No heat signatures were present in the area. No life.

Jacobi spoke up suddenly, shattering the eerie silence. 'Wait, I've got something. Singular life form! About two minutes out.'

Lorna peered through the observation window. 'Ho-ly shit.'

Jacobi looked out eagerly. 'What is it, Cap?'

'A ship.'

'Woah…' Archer breathed, dumbfounded.

The ship looked as though half of it was missing. Space junk floated aimlessly around the wreckage. Some kind of explosion appeared to have destroyed the engine and taken the back half of the ship with it. Something had gone *very wrong* out here.

Lorna looked on in horror. 'How the hell is anyone alive on that thing?'

'I don't know, Cap, but I'm definitely picking someone up,' Jacobi insisted.

'Or some-*thing*,' Archer said, a concerning tone of caution in his voice.

'Shut up, Archer,' Jacobi said, nervously.

Lorna clapped her hands together to get the crew's attention. 'Let's get this show on the road. We're on a time crunch.'

'What's the play, Cap?'

'Set your weapons to stun. I don't want a whole faction after us if we kill one of their own.'

Archer scoffed. 'They've been floating out here for almost two years and we're only picking up one life form. If someone was coming for them, they would've rocked up already.'

Lorna looked at Archer pointedly. 'Set your weapons to stun.' He didn't argue again.

The crew put on their suits, geared up, and loaded into the travel pod. Sweat beaded on Archer's brow while Jacobi began fiddling with the hem of her suit.

Lorna breathed deeply. 'Helmets on. Keep your guard up.'

They docked.

The atmosphere inside the wrecked ship was thick. The air was populated by strange particles that shimmered as they bounced aimlessly around the cabin. The loss of pressure in the area had caused everything that was not secured to join the particles. The crew found themselves dodging medical carts, storage containers, and other wayward supplies.

Lorna came across a strange, organic-like structure. The deep, crystalline, black shard was almost as tall as her. It was a peculiar shape…almost human.

Archer looked at Lorna, baffled. 'What is that?'

'No idea.'

Archer reached out a hand to touch the structure but Lorna caught him and shook her head. Archer nodded silently and let his arm fall back to his side. They kept moving.

The silence was unsettling. The thought that anyone could be alive on this ship was almost impossible to entertain. At one point, Lorna was sure she saw something move along the cabin roof. She'd turned to investigate, but nothing was there. The crew came to a door that separated the destroyed part of the ship from the part still intact. After some heavy resistance, they forced their way in. They waited anxiously as the cabin re-pressurised.

'Helmets stay on, people. We have no way of knowing the status of the oxygen in here.'

Archer spoke up, 'So this weapon, how do we kno—'

A vicious screech ripped through the cabin.

'What the fuck was that?' Archer whipped his head around, horrified.

'Weapons hot. Proceed with caution,' Lorna ordered.

'Proceed? Cap, we should get the fuck out of here!' Archer pleaded.

'Not so keen for the credits now, are we?' Jacobi mocked.

'Screw you, Jacobi,' Archer sneered, still scanning the ship with anxious eyes.

As they pushed further into the ship, Lorna caught sight of a shining metal case with a biohazard symbol printed on the top—the lid was cracked open.

'Shit.' Lorna jogged towards the case and opened it. All that was left inside was a broken glass vial.

'Fuck!' Archer kicked the case. 'So, no credits, and we're on a ship with some fucking monster.'

'Monster is a bit far; we don't know what that was. It could have been a malfunctioning piece of tech for all we know. Plus—' Jacobi stopped suddenly, her eyes wide, her mouth open.

'Jacobi, what is—' A jagged, blade-like object protruded from Jacobi's stomach. Before any of them could react, it ripped itself from Jacobi's abdomen and she fell to the ground, gasping for air.

The crew looked from Jacobi to the thing that stabbed her. It was human…or it had been. Its eyes were gone, and only empty black holes were left behind. Its veins were a midnight black and dark shards leaked from its pores, mixing with coagulated blood. It twitched uncontrollably. The creature opened its mouth, and for a moment Lorna thought it was going to speak, but all it managed was a gurgling sound; several decayed teeth fell from its mouth to the floor. The creature had a particular air about it that suggested to Lorna that her helmet was shielding her from a truly foul smell.

Archer raised his weapon. 'Cap, we've gotta get Jacobi out of here now!'

Lorna readied herself. 'Stun it and we'll grab her.'

The thing stumbled towards them, gnashing its teeth.

'Do it now!' Lorna yelled.

Archer emptied three rounds out of fear. They did nothing.

'What the hell?! It's still coming.'

It collided with Archer, sending them crashing to the ground. 'Get it off me!'

Lorna looked around desperately. She spotted a long piece of metal that appeared to have torn away from the interior hull and grabbed it. She rushed forward and stuck it through the creature's chest, forcing it off Archer.

The creature rolled about the cabin, attempting to pry the metal from its disfigured body. Lorna rushed to Archer.

'Are you hurt?'

Archer hastily assessed himself. 'I'm clear.'

Lorna nodded towards Jacobi. 'Help me with her!'

They each grabbed one of Jacobi's arms and dragged her back the way they came.

As they ran, Lorna heard items being pushed violently around the cabin. The creature had managed to rip the metal from its flesh. Inhuman screams filled the halls as it chased them.

'It's gaining on us, Cap. We're not gonna make it!'

Lorna chanced a glance behind them and saw that

Archer was right.

'There! That door isn't locked.'

They crashed into the room, tripping on a cargo container, and fell to the floor in a heap. Jacobi groaned in pain. Archer desperately rose and made for the door's control panel. Just as it locked, the creature ran into it and started banging incessantly. Archer slid to the ground, his back still to the door. 'We're so fucked.'

'Archer, you need to keep your head.'

Archer began hyperventilating and crawled across the cold floor towards Jacobi. He propped her up against some cargo and began trying to dress her wounds.

'You're gonna be okay. It's alright.'

Jacobi coughed, taking in a wheezy breath. 'I don't feel good.' Tears began forming in her eyes.

Archer grabbed her face. 'Hey, look at me. You're gonna get through this. Who's gonna annoy the shit out of me if you aren't around, huh? Just focus on your breathing.'

He looked desperately to Lorna, 'We need to get her back to the *Malum*.'

Lorna nodded, trying to pull herself together. 'This is the security room. If we can activate something that makes a lot of noise, it might draw the creature away. Help me look.' She began scanning the monitors.

Archer gave Jacobi a reassuring look. 'I'll be just over there, okay? We'll get you home.'

Jacobi nodded weakly.

The creature continued to throw itself against the door, showing no signs of fatigue. After a few minutes of uneasy searching, Archer spoke up. 'Uh… Cap, you're gonna wanna see this.'

'What is it?' Lorna walked over to stand beside Archer.

He rewound the security footage and let it play. It showed a member of the ship's crew, alive and well. He was carrying a case. The man stopped in a quiet part of the ship and looked around cautiously. He set the case down and punched in a code, causing it to spring open.

'Idiot!' Archer exclaimed.

Lorna and Archer's heads whipped towards the door as the creature screeched and began hitting the door with more ferocity.

'Quiet,' Lorna warned. Archer nodded.

The crew member extracted a vial and held it up for inspection. Then suddenly, his head snapped to the side as if he'd heard something, and the vial hit the floor, smashing into pieces. The matter wove across the ground, surrounding the man's feet. It crawled up his legs as he panicked and yelled for help. At that moment, as if a switch had been flicked, the matter forced itself into every pore of the man's skin. It slithered inside his nose and his eyes, making its way to his ears. He fell to the ground, writhing in pain. His limbs began to rapidly decay. His flesh fell from his body and was replaced by obsidian-like formations. For a moment, Lorna and Archer watched as the man lay still on the floor. Then, after a few moments, he rose. Black liquid was pouring from his skin, as if there wasn't enough room inside his body to hold it all. He was exploding from the inside out. He twitched uncontrollably. Gun shots could be heard as someone out of frame fired in the man's direction, attempting to incapacitate him. He ran forwards and the only thing Lorna could see was a pool of blood entering the frame.

'That's why Maverick told us not to let the weapon come into physical contact with us,' Lorna realised.

A loud bang reverberated throughout the small room, causing Lorna to jump. She looked towards the door and saw a large dent.

Archer looked to Lorna in terror.

'But how the hell did he know?' he whispered.

'He said he had an informant. Maybe someone made it off the ship?'

Archer laughed in a sour tone. 'Yeah, right.'

Another loud bang.

Lorna looked to the door with concern, and then back to Archer. 'I really need you to keep your shit together here. We aren't going to make it out of this if we don't do it together. Is there anything else you can find?'

Archer breathed deeply, refocusing himself. He scanned through the records, then hesitated. 'There's an outgoing transmission. But it's a private broadcast, sent to a solitary user.'

Lorna took a deep breath. 'Play it.'

Archer hit a button and a woman's face popped up on the screen. She was dishevelled and afraid.

'This is Commander Adams,' she stated weakly. 'I'm sending you this message to tell you that the crew has been exposed to the matter.' She paused and sniffled. 'I'm the only one left alive. They've all…they mutated, turned into monsters. When you gave us this weapon to transport to Commercium, you should've…why didn't you warn us? You killed my crew, you bastard!' Black liquid leaked from the woman's nose. 'And now you've killed me.'

The transmission ended.

Archer slowly turned towards Lorna. She shook her head, finally understanding.

'Commercium?' Archer questioned.

Lorna looked at him. 'Can you see who the transmission was sent to?' She hoped her instincts were wrong.

Archer began typing and then smashed the desk with his fist, walking away from the monitor with his head in his hands. Lorna stared at the screen, a pit forming in her stomach.

Time: Transmitted at 21:04 hours

…

Location: Commercium

…

Recipient: Mr Maverick Wolfe

…

Transmission status: Unknown

'He knew,' Archer yelled. 'He fucking knew.'

'Keep it down!' Lorna whispered.

Archer shrunk beneath her gaze and began pacing. 'That fucker sent us to our deaths! When we get out of here, I'm gonna—'

Lorna interrupted, 'He didn't know everything.'

'What's that supposed to mean?'

Lorna checked the monitor to confirm. 'It says the transmission status is unknown. I doubt Maverick ever received this. Why would he send us? He wants the weapon intact. If he knew it had broken containment, he wouldn't have sent us. It wouldn't make any sense.'

Archer still looked confused, 'But *why* does he want the weapon?'

'Your guess is as good as mine. I say we get Jacobi back to the ship and get her some medical attention. We'll haul ass to Commercium and—'

A gurgling sound reverberated around the room, like someone choking on blood. Lorna turned, remembering that they had propped Jacobi up against the wall in the corner of the room. Now, she was standing.

'Jacobi, are you alright?' Lorna stepped towards her.

Jacobi raised her head and Lorna screamed. Jacobi's eyes were gone. All that was left were two empty voids, oozing with thick black liquid. Her teeth were cracked, parts of them falling from her mouth and rolling around the inside of her visor. Her skin started sagging from the weight of the fluid building up inside her system. Lorna froze in horror, her eyes welling with tears. Jacobi took an unsteady step forward.

'Jacobi,' Archer pleaded, 'you're still in there, please—'

Jacobi gnashed her teeth and began desperately scratching at her visor, trying to remove it. She was becoming more agitated by the second.

Archer took a step forward, 'Let me he—'

Jacobi let out a blood-curdling cry and violently smashed her head against the cabin wall. Lorna and Archer stood in shock. Jacobi's visor smashed. Some shards fell to the ground while others became lodged in Jacobi's eye sockets and cheeks.

'That's enough, Jacobi!' Lorna pleaded.

Jacobi's head snapped towards Lorna. She screamed, causing a waterfall of black matter to spill from her decaying mouth, then she lunged.

Archer pushed Lorna to the side as he crashed to the ground with Jacobi on top of him. She latched onto his shoulder with blackened teeth and began tearing flesh from his body. As Archer screamed in agony, Lorna reacted quickly, rising from the ground and retrieving a long metal pipe from the floor. She pulled it back and swung it full force into Jacobi's head. It was enough to get her off Archer. He crawled backwards, using his good hand to hold his arm together. Jacobi regained her footing and lunged for Archer again, but Lorna ran forward. She skewered Jacobi with the pipe and drove it into the wall, trapping her. Jacobi clawed at Lorna. There was no sign of the friend she once knew. Jacobi was dead.

Lorna grabbed Archer and pulled him to his feet; she found an old piece of tarp amongst the cargo and wrapped his shoulder with it. 'We need to go, now!'

Archer shook his head. 'Sorry, Cap. I'm not coming with you.'

Lorna was confused. 'What?'

'How do you think the rest of the crew got infected?' He nodded to his shoulder.

Already Lorna could see the black matter writhing within his flesh. She bowed her head.

'It's okay, Cap,' he reassured. 'I've got you covered. Just get back to the ship and make sure Wolfe pays.' He paused, giving Lorna's arm a reassuring squeeze. 'Tell my little one that I love her. She needs to know how much I love her.'

Archer let go and walked towards the door, where the creature was still pounding with all its weight.

'Archer, don't!' Lorna pleaded.

But he had made his choice.

'Run,' he said. He opened the door and tackled the creature to the ground. Lorna watched in horror as they rolled about the cabin. 'Go!' Archer screamed. Lorna ran until she reached the door separating the two sections of the ship and hit the button. She heard Archer scream in pain…and the door closed.

Lorna went back to her ship alone. She stripped off her suit and exhaustedly made her way to her quarters.

She sat in front of her monitor and looked down at her arm. She saw four long, blackened scratch marks, something left behind from her fight with Jacobi. It was only a matter of time now.

Lorna took a long, shaky breath, and turned on the camera. She found the military channel and started the transmission.

'This is Captain Lorna of the SS *Malum*. My crew and I were hired to retrieve an unknown weapon from the twelfth sector. We came to find out that the weapon was some form of matter. When it comes into contact with a human, it transforms them into mindless, vicious monsters. It takes mere minutes to transform someone you know into something unrecognisable. I lost my team…my friends.' She paused. 'I've been exposed. Don't come for me, there will be nothing but death waiting for you. In the city of Commercium, there is a shop by the name of Wolfe's Intergalactic Antiquities. Antiquities are not the only thing Maverick Wolfe deals in. He organised the transportation of this weapon and has indirectly murdered two entire crews. I don't know what he planned to do with the matter, but he'll never have it. Find him. Find him and make him pay. Captain Lorna out.'

Lorna looked once again at the wound on her arm. Black shards pushed their way further into her body. She could feel them cutting her flesh apart from the inside. Blood vessels burst and muscles were torn apart—*agony*. A few shards fell from her arm and floated into the ship's ventilation system. Lorna lent to the side and retrieved a case she'd grabbed from medical on her way to her quarters. She opened it to find a singular vial and needle. The vial was filled with a clear, glossy liquid. She attached the vial to the needle and gently pressed it into her arm, injecting the entirety of the fluid into her bloodstream.

As Lorna sat in her quarters, losing consciousness, she felt a sense of peace. Peace from knowing that the infection would not be passed on through her…that Maverick would lose. As life began to leave her and keeping her eyes open became impossible, she heard the crackle of a radio.

'Captain Lorna, this is Colonel J. Williams. We're receiving you, but your signal is faint and we can't make everything out. Hold tight, help is on the way.'

Lorna screamed, but no sound came out. She tried to reach for the monitor, but her body wouldn't move. *No, no, no.*

Every morsel of peace she had felt in her last moments was ripped away.

The Wolf and the Songbird

Rose Star

The roads and fields were still slightly soft from melted snow, but in the forest the ground held firm, supported by the roots of the trees and other plants that grew within. My hooves traversed the familiar path as it wound upwards, until I was able to see my village from the mountainside. Our little stone cottages were tucked into a clearing in the forest, smoke rising from their chimneys.

The forest was the pride and joy of my people. Many years ago, when the first fauns discovered the valley, it was barren and lifeless. We alone had managed to coax the seeds from the ground again. According to the stories, the valley had been bled dry by a tyrant king a long time ago. Supposedly, he would return one day, but no one truly believed that. Fauns are a community-minded people, without wars or armed conflict, so it was hard to imagine anything disturbing that peace.

The path grew steeper, and the trees sparser. Finally, the ground levelled out, and a stone tower rose ahead.

The ancient castle was long forgotten, reduced to lines of stone covered in brambles that I scrambled over with ease. The tower alone had survived the weathering of hundreds of years. In that time, an oak tree had sprouted at its base, and grown to a mighty size, twined around the tower as if to shelter the stone from the elements.

Up I went, my hooves and hands well accustomed to the route. As I climbed higher, I could hear the gentle sound of singing winding its way down through the leaves. Finally, I reached a thick branch about halfway up the tree, which I shimmied across carefully. Midway along, I was directly in front of an archway in the tower, the only window or entrance I had ever found.

Golden light shone out from the window. A canopied bed stood in one corner of the room, with a bookshelf full of leather-bound tomes next to it. The only other furnishings were a wooden table with a single chair and a rug on the floor. A girl sat alone by the fireplace, carefully combing her hair as she sang.

'Mira,' I called softly, perching comfortably on the wide branch. She looked up and bounced over to the window.

'Robin! I hoped you would come soon. I've been terribly bored.'

'I brought you a gift,' I said, bracing myself to hand her a small bunch of flowers. She leaned out of the window and took them from me gently. 'The first flowers of spring.'

Long ago when I'd first discovered Mira, I had tried to enter the tower through the window. But when I did, I found myself alone in the empty, derelict ruins of a tower room, floor rotten and crumbling under my hooves. Mira couldn't fully cross the windowsill either, as if she was attached to the tower by a rope. She would only ever say she was imprisoned, but not why. I didn't press her.

She wrinkled her nose. 'Thank you,' she said, taking the flowers and laying them aside immediately. She was in the same pale blue dress as always, which never seemed to get dirty or torn. 'What news do you have?'

I ignored the blunt greeting. Her way of talking seemed discourteous if you didn't know her, but I had gotten used to it. Sometimes it made me wonder if she'd ever truly had a friend before. Either way, I suspected she was desperately lonely now, and so I kept coming back.

'Nothing from outside our village,' I said, fiddling with the ring that hung around my neck. 'The snow has started melting here, but the passes are still blocked.'

Mira hummed distractedly, picking the petals off one of the bright yellow flowers I had brought her.

'So you haven't met anyone strange lately?' It was the two questions she asked me every visit, and so far, my answers had never seemed to satisfy her.

'You're the only non-faun I've seen since the first snow,' I told her. She nodded once.

Two weeks later, I was in the forest collecting the herbs which had already pushed their way out of the soil. Straightening up from a promising patch, I heard a woman's voice. Curious, I wandered back towards the road.

Across the narrow path, a pedlar's cart stood crookedly. Pots, pans, shoes, lanterns, and other assorted household items hung on pegs driven into the side. An old woman stomped around the wagon, uttering a string of curse words as she went. Her garments were tattered, little more than a series of patches sewn neatly together. One of her gnarled fingers had a golden ring, a bright contrast to the other mundane and somewhat shabby items around her. The only other living creature in sight was a bluebird in a golden cage, hanging at the front of the wagon.

'Do you need help?' I asked, stepping forward. The woman jerked in surprise, swinging her wooden cane to point at me. I raised my hands to show I was no threat, and she lowered it slowly.

'Yes, I do,' she said grumpily. 'The damn harness broke, and now my donkey has run off to gods-know-where. As if it wasn't enough being lost.' She scowled. 'The damn mountains themselves have changed since I was last here.'

My eyebrows rose. 'Perhaps I can help you?' I offered. 'I'm sure your donkey can't have gotten far.'

'Even if I get him back, there's not much use he can be with a broken harness,' the woman grumbled, eyes taking me in. 'But you're welcome to try.'

Following the flight of a wayward donkey was hardly difficult, especially for a faun. It was barely half an hour later that I stepped back onto the road where the woman was, donkey in tow.

'Now, let me look at that harness,' I said.

The woman watched me from under her bushy, grey eyebrows as I investigated the broken harness. It was just a snapped strap, easily replaceable.

'I'll be back soon,' I promised her, and started towards home.

I returned with the leather and tools I needed and fashioned a new strap. The sun had begun its descent before I stood up and declared my work complete.

'I thank you, stranger,' the woman said. 'But there is one more thing I need. There should be ruins in this valley. Where are they?'

'Northwest of here,' I said automatically, and then wondered if that could endanger Mira. Although, sizing the woman up, I decided she probably wouldn't be able to climb the tree. 'They aren't far.'

The woman nodded. 'Three times you have offered your help freely. I shall not let you go unrewarded.' Her voice took on a strange resonance, and her eyes flashed gold. 'For the donkey you returned to me, you may ask for any possession I currently own. For the strap you fixed, you may ask me to complete any task for you that is within my power. And finally, for your directions, you may ask me any question and I will answer it to the best of my knowledge. Hear me and know I am bound to these promises.'

I stepped back, eyes wide. 'You're a witch.'

'I'm a pedlar,' said the woman unconvincingly. 'Why don't you have a look at the goods in my wagon and pick something out?'

'No need,' I said. 'I want the bird in the cage there. Animals should be free.'

She scowled. 'Not that. Anything but that.'

'I thought you were bound to your promise?' I countered, eyebrow raised. 'You said anything of yours, and I want the bird.'

'It is not mine to give,' the woman snapped. 'Choose something else.'

I set my mouth in a stubborn line, but getting into an argument with a probable witch seemed unwise.

'Very well,' I said, looking dubiously over the visible fry pans and blankets. 'But I want its equal.'

A strange look crossed the woman's face, but she nodded, and disappeared into the cart. I heard sounds of clattering, and a 'Dammit, I know I have it somewhere.'

Looking over at the cart in curiosity, my eye caught sight of a blue feather on the ground beneath the birdcage. Picking it up, I tucked it into the leather band around the base of my horn. Perhaps it could be a gift for Mira later.

The pedlar emerged with a silver, hand-held mirror.

'It's enchanted to show you the true nature of

things,' she said, handing it to me. 'I can promise that you'll find it equal to what you asked for.'

I took it gingerly and turned it over. It reflected my face as I had always known it, though with a golden glow by my horn. I wondered at that, but I was more interested in the ring around my neck, a family heirloom from my great-grandfather's travels.

'My necklace is a key?' I asked in surprise.

'Hmm?'

I gestured at where it sat at the base of my throat. 'This ring. The mirror reflects it as a key. Why?'

'Oh.' The woman looked surprised. 'It's a common thing in some regions to hide keys as ordinary objects. Rings are popular because they're portable.'

I blinked and decided to ask my grandmother if she knew anything about it.

'You still have a task to give me and a question to ask,' the woman pointed out. I thought for a moment.

'Do I have to choose them now?'

The pedlar sighed. 'I will be here for three days. You have until midnight on the third.'

I struggled to sleep that night, thinking of the pedlar's promises. What could I possibly want from her? After my morning meal, I set out for the ruins.

When I got there, the pedlar was nowhere to be found. Shrugging, I started my ascent of the tree.

'Mira,' I called when I got to the top, but she was already at the window.

'Back so soon?' she asked, eyebrow raised. 'Do you bring news?'

'I met a witch claiming to not be a witch yesterday,' I told her, settling in my usual spot. 'I helped her, and in exchange she gave me three gifts.'

A perturbed look crossed her face. 'What were they?'

'That I could ask for any item of hers, that I could ask her to do anything for me, and that I could ask any question of her.'

Mira didn't respond, so I added, 'She had a bird with her in a golden cage. I asked for it, but she said it wasn't hers to give.'

At that, Mira looked up suddenly, eyes piercing. 'What did she give you instead?'

'A mirror that can show me the true nature of things.'

'Do you have the mirror with you?'

I shook my head, and she scowled for the briefest moment.

'I want to see it.'

'I'll bring it on my next visit,' I said equitably. 'In the meantime, I can't decide what to ask for. Any ideas?'

Mira looked past me, face wistful. 'I know what I would ask.'

'Tell me.'

'Well, if she actually was a witch, then she might be able to release me from this tower.'

I sat up straighter. 'Of course! I'll ask that, then.'

The woman wasn't difficult to find, as her wagon left deep grooves in the ground. I followed them from the road where I had met her and finally found the clearing where she had camped. The donkey was tethered to a tree, attempting to eat a bush that was just out of reach.

The pedlar was sitting on a small stool by a fire, cutting onions for the cauldron of soup in front of her. She looked up as I arrived.

'Ah, if it isn't the intrepid young faun. Have you decided what you would have me do?'

I took a deep breath. 'There is a woman trapped in the tower that stands in the ruins. Is it within your power to free her?'

The pedlar was silent for a long while, staring at the tree beside me. Finally, she bowed her head. 'It is.'

'Release her then.'

She took a deep breath. 'I would beg you to reconsider. Anything but that.'

'That is my choice,' I said firmly. 'People should be imprisoned least of all.'

The pedlar closed her eyes tight, then opened them again. 'Very well. It is a full moon tonight. I will do it at the stroke of midnight. You cannot be here.'

I opened my mouth to protest, but she shook her head.

'That is my condition. You *must not be here*. Understand?'

I closed my mouth and nodded.

The next morning, I rose early and hurried up to the ruins, only stopping to eat and grab the little silver mirror to show Mira.

The tower had been flattened. Blackened stones were strewn about the ruins, crushing moss and ferns where they lay. The big oak tree that had entwined it was alive, though it looked more battered and gnarled than it had before. A single bluebird warbled prettily from its branches. Neither Mira nor the pedlar were anywhere to be seen.

I searched the ruins for anything to show what had happened, but there was nothing. Sighing in defeat, I sat at the foot of the great oak tree and took out the silver mirror to fiddle with. Raising it up, I stared morosely at myself.

The old pedlar was behind me.

With a yell of surprise, I leapt away from the tree and spun to face her.

There was no one there.

I looked in the mirror again and saw only myself and the forest behind me. Slowly, I turned my back to the oak tree, and tried again.

The woman stood there, where the tree had been.

I stumbled and nearly tripped over a root in surprise. Slowly and carefully, I backed up towards the tree, keeping the woman in sight. Narrowing my eyes, I considered my next action very carefully.

'You still owe me a question,' I told her.

The wind sighed through the branches in agreement.

'Who are you?'

The branches creaked, but no responses were forthcoming. I leaned back against the broad trunk and waited.

The sun rose above the trees to where I lay. Lulled by the warmth, I fell asleep.

And then I dreamed.

I was inside Mira's tower, in front of the bookcase. My hands reached for a book, which then flew open at me. Words leapt out from the page.

Once upon a time, there was a princess who lived in a golden castle.

Outside the walls, the world was cold, and the fields often lay barren. But the princess suffered none of that, for her father ensured she had enough to eat and as many blankets as she needed to stay warm.

Another girl, whose father was also the king, lived in the castle. She was not a princess but instead a lowly servant's bastard. Her bed was cold, and her meals were scant.

In time, the princess grew and needed a companion. The girl who was not a princess was chosen, and suddenly she had enough to eat and was warm at night. The princess laughed at how much she ate and nicknamed her Wolf for her hunger. She did not say it kindly. Wolf learned how to smile even when she wanted to grit her teeth, and how to say nice things when she just wanted to scream.

The girls grew bigger, and the kingdom grew hungrier. The king was worried, for he felt the simmering anger of his people. He hired a witch to teach the princess magic so that she might protect herself. He made Wolf learn too, so she might protect the princess.

In time, the king passed, and the princess became a queen. She looked at the starving people of her kingdom and laughed, for she did not care. She taxed them ever more ruthlessly, just to show that she could, as she thought them powerless.

She was wrong.

Her father's fears came true sooner than he had expected. A year into her reign, a mob arrived at the castle walls with torches and angry, hungry faces. The soldiers did not stop them, for they too were hungry.

The queen fled into the tower at the centre of the castle, and begged Wolf to keep her safe. Wolf obliged, and used her magic to seal the queen within, where no one could ever harm her. She would never grow old, or suffer the pangs of hunger, or feel cold. And she was a prisoner there, as long as Wolf still lived.

Wolf walked away from the smoking ruins with a golden cage, a ring on her finger, and a songbird. Beneath her feet, the barren land yielded its first, green sprout.

And she smiled.

I woke with a start, the afternoon sun casting long shadows ahead of me. Above me, the big oak tree rustled agitatedly in the wind.

Mira stood in front of me, her own shadow streaming long behind her. She clasped her hands in front of herself, golden hair falling loose around her shoulders. On one finger was a wooden ring, which seemed oddly out of place with her blue silk dress. I stared at it and thought of the single golden ring and the princess in the golden cage.

'You never did tell me why you were in that tower,' I said slowly, standing up.

She shrugged prettily. 'Does it matter? I'm out now. Aren't you glad?'

'Strangely enough, it does matter.'

She sighed. 'This used to be my castle, countless years ago now. A servant betrayed me and trapped me when a mob attacked the castle.'

I swallowed.

'The tyrant king brought many years' barrenness to this valley, even after his castle was destroyed,' I recited in horror. 'Some say he'll one day return.'

'Not him, but his daughter,' Mira said matter-of-factly, then her face twisted in spite. 'Now that you've finally released me, I shall destroy everything that servant—that *animal* loved, starting with this valley.'

I stared, shocked. 'You have no power, no connections—'

Mira clicked her fingers and lighting struck a nearby sapling, causing it to burst into flames with an eerie blue tint to them.

'I can do whatever I want with my magic.' She smiled. 'It's all thanks to you, really. When your kind are toiling in the fields growing my crops, you alone may stay by my side. Foreign nobles will be fascinated by my faun pet, I am sure.'

I recoiled in horror. Our natural ways of life were so free. The thought of the valley turning into the land in my dream was unbearable.

I narrowed my eyes and took a deep breath. 'You admit you owe me your freedom,' I said, keeping my voice steady. 'I would ask you for one small thing in exchange.'

'Very well. I suppose you wish for riches? Or power in my court?'

'No, nothing so important. I only wish for the wooden ring you wear now.'

Her other hand flew to cover it. 'No. Not that,' she said flatly.

'I insist. Surely you don't want to start your new kingdom with a debt to pay?'

She stared at me, delicate nostrils flaring. 'Fine,' she spat, wrenching the ring off and throwing it at my feet. 'It's not like you can do much with it anyway.'

I picked it up gently and slipped it on. It was cool

and polished. Above me, the leaves of the ancient oak tree rustled slightly.

Hoping my guess was right, I held up my hand in front of the mirror. In the glass, I held a wooden key.

I stepped forward to the trunk of the tree.

'What are you doing?' Mira asked frantically.

I ignored her. Using the mirror, I searched the smooth trunk until I found what I was looking for.

A keyhole.

I moved my hand towards it, but Mira leapt towards me, grabbing my arm and pushing it away from the tree. I pushed back, and to my relief, I was stronger. Slowly, my hand inched towards the keyhole. Finally, I pressed my hand against the spot and closed my eyes. A loud crack sounded and, when I opened my eyes again, the old pedlar stood in front of me.

Mira gave a cry of dismay.

'I find myself once more in your debt,' Wolf said, nodding her head at me. 'I am unsure how to repay you.'

'I know how,' I told her. 'I have no wish for this valley to become a kingdom again. Help me stop that from happening and I'll consider your debt paid.'

Panic flashed across Mira's face before she recovered herself. 'Sister dearest, I've missed you,' she said, stepping over to Wolf.

Wolf raised her grey eyebrows. 'You trapped me in a tree, *sister*.'

'And you locked me in a tower for an age!' Mira

shouted, then took a deep breath. 'And besides, I just locked your physical body inside the tree. Both of us know your true self.'

I looked between them. 'What?'

Mira smiled sweetly. 'To prolong her life, she trapped her soul in an oak tree. As long as the tree lives, so does she. And what better way to guard me?' She reached up and made as if to touch Wolf's face and then pouted, drawing her hand back.

'Unfortunately, it doesn't stop you from ageing as the tree does. She's bent and gnarled, where I'm still young and fresh.' She laughed. 'Thank you for that at least, sister.'

Wolf snarled. 'I will lock you back up if it is my final action. I've learned more since I was the scared little girl forced to be your subject, Queen Kasmira.'

Mira smiled, ever so sweetly. 'And how are you going to manage that? You have no hold over me, and I will do everything in my power to stop you getting one.'

I opened my mouth and then closed it again. 'Wolf,' I said slowly, taking the blue feather out from where it still lay next to my horn. 'Would this help?'

Wolf and Mira both stared at me.

'Where did you get this?' Wolf asked suspiciously.

'It was on the ground under the birdcage,' I replied. 'I picked it up when you were inside the wagon.'

Mira clenched her fists, and fire appeared in them. 'Give that to me,' she hissed through her teeth.

The wind picked up and the leaves around me flew into the air, creating a wall between Mira and me.

'You know where the wagon is,' Wolf called to me, hands open flat. 'Run to it now and put the feather in the golden cage. I can hold her off.'

I nodded and bolted instantly, my hoofs not faltering for a second on the uneven ground. Behind me I heard yelling, but I did not look back. Either I made it, or all was lost.

Across rotten leaves I sped, and over roots and fallen branches I leapt. Trees loomed in the way, but I danced between them without thought. Brambles reared up in front of me, and I jumped over them, the thick hide of my legs withstanding their thorns. Behind me, a storm started.

Finally, I burst into the clearing where the pedlar's wagon stood. The golden cage hung at the front, though the door was open and there was no bird to be seen. I lifted my hand which still clutched the bright blue, slightly tattered feather.

And then I hesitated. I was about to go against everything my people believed in and imprison a living creature. It prevented a greater evil, but that would not change the morality of my own decision.

A deafening crack sounded from the direction of the ruins. Hastily, I thrust the feather inside the cage and shut the door, dropping the pin home. Then I screwed my eyes shut and tried to breathe deeply.

When I opened them, the cage held a small, blue bird, its claws stained with blood. I held up my mirror with a shaking hand and turned so I could see the cage's reflection. Resolutely, I ignored the new golden ring on my finger.

Mira stared reproachfully at me from behind the bars, looking the same as the friend I had known in the tower. Her hands were coated in scarlet blood which dripped slowly onto her bright blue dress. Sickened, I turned away, and ran with a heavy heart back towards the ruins.

Wolf lay slumped against the trunk of the great oak tree, clutching a bloodied hand to her torso. The oak tree itself had a gaping hole in the side of it, and I knew it would not survive. Perhaps both were already dead because of my hesitation.

When I fell to my knees next to her, she opened her eyes and gave me a genuine smile. 'Well done,' she whispered.

I frantically started tearing strips from my shirt for bandages, tears forming in my eyes. 'How do I help you?'

'You can't. The tree will die in three days, and I will pass with it.' Wolf took a deep breath and winced. 'You have already helped me by trapping Kasmira.'

I shook my head vehemently. 'Won't she be released when you die?'

'No. You put her in the cage yourself, so now you are her warden.' Wolf took another painful breath. 'Guard her well, little one.'

I looked down at the golden ring on my finger and shuddered.

I went back for the donkey and used him to carry Wolf into the village. The cage I carried myself in secret, and I put it in the darkest part of my cellar, along with the mirror. I told the village what had happened, though I made it sound as though Mira had died. Wolf was given food and a soft bed and all the comforts that we fauns could conjure to show our gratitude. When she died, I took her body and buried it under the sapling of a new oak tree.

The golden cage stood alone in my basement, with no one around to hear the song of the little blue bird within.

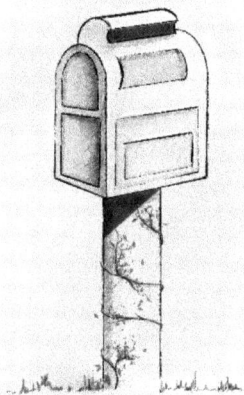

How to Outdo your Parents

Cara Migalka

First: Learn to compare.

Grow up thinking they're old fashioned, too cheap to upgrade. Feel embarrassed by teak panelled record player, giant speakers, and album rack below. Wish you had a shiny, black all-in-one, like Paul up the road. Scour a Le Cornu's catalogue that the pushbike kid leaves halfway out of the letterbox. Cringe at said letterbox because Dad's quirky manner propels him to salvage a red post box with the old-style keyhole, paint it white, and mount it on a concrete stand. Think, how much mail are you expecting, but know better than to criticise Dick. Puzzle over how Dad's name, Richard, became Dick. Pray your inherited name won't befall a similar fate. Show Mum the glossy pictures, explain how the twin tub has evolved. Endure a water conservation lecture and wish you'd never broached the subject. Drop hints to Dad that TVs now have colour. Predict his response, where money doesn't grow, and decipher why beggars can't be choosers.

Adopt panic-face when friends come knocking. Call, 'I'll be right out,' concerned they'll think it's your dead grandmother's house. Receive a dead arm from older brother for making collages of interior design. Dream about the day your puny stick-arms will build up and pin him to the ground. Imagine being born into a different family, more like Laura's, with dogs, a sister, and a velour modular lounge.

Earn your own money at fourteen flipping burgers in polyester pants with a matching cap. Resent Dick for declaring you now owe him twenty dollars for a thing called 'board'. Slide your pay-packet and passbook to the teller on Fridays. Admire both the red stamps filling the pages and the gold buttons on his navy-blue uniform. Aspire to be a tie-bearing, uniform-wearing, gold-buttoned clerk.

Then: Consume endlessly.

Compete ruthlessly for entry-level-corporate. Claw your way from team leader to middle management. Assume superiority because your employment now warrants a suit. Commit to a thirty-year debt for a home of your own. Replicate the interior from the display village in Sunrise Estate. Invite your parents over and show off the flat pack décor. Bang on about the price. Offer to take them to the homemaker centre, redo their place. Puzzle at the refusal of such a generous proposal. Visit them in your childhood home and sit stiffly in the ungiving chesterfield. Encourage them to live a little, loosen the purse strings. Mock their secure term deposit. Educate them on the borrowing power of equity in their paid-off home. Fail to mention your portfolio anxiety and a market downturn on the ASX.

Purchase another house because one is never enough. Contribute to the rental crisis by listing BnBs in the sky. Upgrade repeatedly, cars, partners, junk. Abandon pineapple phase for white pot plants. Reframe all your prints, have them done in a slim neutral-toned wood. Replace your black leather Eames replica recliner and matching ottoman with a white linen sofa. Wonder how you ever thought boho cushions were attractive. Convince yourself, this next thing will bring the happiness you seek. Despair that the exhilaration is fleeting.

Forsake homewares and take up travel. Endure extended flights to exotic locations. Delude yourself you are supporting decimated economies. Over-eat, over-drink, over-shop. Under-give.

Then: The uncomfortable truth.

Wheel your mum, Barbara, through a maze of hospital corridors. Find Oncologist—Clinic A. Speak to a disgruntled receptionist shielded by Perspex. Watch Barb struggle with the zip on her bag with the red butterflies. Hand over her Medicare card and hear the wait time is forty-five minutes. Scan rows of plastic seating and choose one with at least a three-seat gap. Remind yourself, cancer's not contagious—but still. Back the wheelchair in front of the chair next to you. Observe Mum's pink scalp through thinning hair. Envisage yourself aging and plunge into existential crisis. Divert panic attack by focusing on the waiting room. Sympathise with the exhausted laminate and misery-scarred paint. Check out the people staring straight ahead, open-eyed with an inward gaze. Distract yourself with The Morning Show playing on a large screen attached to the wall. Read bold type on the corner of the screen, 'How to level up your fajitas.' Watch a chef in oversized earrings, red glasses, and bold prints mix chicken strips into spice. Read closed captions.

'They're great, those premixed seasonings.'

'Well, I think it's tastier.'

'What we love about your recipes is that they are budget-friendly.'

Whisper to Mum, 'Do you want a coffee?' Argue that forty-five minutes is enough time. Spot Mum's white fingertips gripping her butterflies. Turn back to fajitas.

Note the white-coated doctors materialising at the end of a hallway. Hear names released into the air and wait to see where they land. Watch people stand and guess, who's going to die? Retell yourself—we all are. Notice the loved ones walk a heartbeat behind, holding files or lightly touching elbows. Think, support person, then Google support on your phone. Read, 'to bear all or part of the weight.' Protest it's all, and where the hell is your brother? Recognise your surname breaking the silence. Acknowledge the woman with waist-long, satin hair, her silky blouse tucked into a pencil skirt. Follow the click of stilettos to the consulting room. Think, slay but also, what kinda work shoe is that? Remain conflicted because Grey's Anatomy is your favourite series, but this is reality. Hate that Mum's in the public system, a guinea pig for baby doctors. Remember being the first to diss health insurance and debating with your friends, 'If there's an accident, you're going to the closest hospital regardless.' Regret that you didn't consider that some accidents are slow moving.

Then: The uncharted wilderness.

Spend extra time with Dad. Allow space for him to reminisce, process the trauma of war. Suspect his stories are being confused with those he has been told. Dig out the black and white photos; a young man full of promise, a pretty wife by his side. Catch a flash of clarity and ride its bloom with enthused agreeance. Sense the wilting hope as clouds roll in. Remind him again that your name is also Richard and no, Mum's not coming home. Feel grateful that death came to him in sleep—that it wasn't you that found him.

Force your brother to fly in from interstate to help. Drag fridge and washer to the roadside. Write 'free' on cardboard in thick black ink. Salvage Tupperware and ancient cooking appliances from the backs of cupboards. Remain fair and business-like—for all of two hours. Dodge a lettuce spinner tossed at your head. Watch the lid roll off to the laundry like a runaway wheel. Refer to him as 'F' ending in 'head'. Surprise yourself with the swiftness your twelve-year-old self reappeared. Take offence at his homophobic retort. Absolve him of any further duties.

Call Wolfe's Antiques to appraise remaining items. Snort at his insulting offer. Resolve to deal with it yourself. Ponder the quandary of limited space. Hire a storage unit not far from your home. Bitch every month you could be feeding a small horse. Wonder why Dick insisted on comparing the price of goods with horse feeding. Spit-it with U-Store and opt for closure. Raise the roller door and stare at the past. Load up the trailer and transport it to the collectables fair.

Off-load onto blue tarp and sit in a camping chair behind a folding card table. Greet browsers and watch their faces light up with recognition. Hear stories of grandparents, musical lolly jars, and a 'fob watch just like that'. Consider an offer on the knife with the carved bone handle. Smell a Sunday roast with salty, crispy beef fat. See Dad swishing the knife along a steel and shaving thin cuts of meat. Slide elbows off the table in reflexive response to memory. Wonder when children stopped asking to leave the table or if they even sit at them anymore. Return knife to its velvet lined box with a gold clasp and place out of view. Respond to query about the drinks cabinet, crafted in solid oak. Demonstrate how the door opens, hinged on the horizontal like a drawbridge. Recall the clink of crystal glasses, sweet smelling port, and asking for a taste. Feel your dad's pat on the head as he laughs, 'Not yet, Son'. Tell the buyer his offer is too low. Watch the lady in a red coat run her hand over the black marble clock. Remember how you once thought it magical, like the one in the Enid Blyton book. Open the gold-rimmed glass door and show her how to wind the hands. Admire the way it sits flat, the marble curving over the top like an admiral's hat. Smile at her attempt to lift it and her surprise at its weight. Toss Mum's blanket of crocheted squares over it. Allow time to reconsider. Haggle with a moustached man over the white marble Egyptian head. Tell him how it came from Cairo on your parent's journey from

England. Discover he had a similar passage of three months on a ship. Suffer through the history of 'ten-pound-poms' and the government migrant scheme. Drift back to your early years, homes surrounded by paddocks, your neighbours all passengers from the same boat. Contemplate the irony of them later demanding to 'stop the boats.' Try to recall where those Polaroid slides went, the ones featuring a grandad you never knew. Rifle through the box with the film cameras. Retrieve both projector and slides and place them by the boot of your car.

Next: Piercing the veil.

Decide on a garage sale and advertise in the local rag. Spend entire weekend waiting for dribs of shoppers and drabs of coin. Despair that your driveway is still full. Hear about the gifting economy, Buy-Nothing, Give-Freely, Swap, Borrow, and Share. Snap photos, crop them, post them online. Emphasise the dismantling will not be done by you. Reflect on wasted hours assembling bolt C with bolt D. Re-live the frustration of missing the crucial step—long screw E. Honour the 'let it simmer approach', the opposite of first in first served. Sift through the flood of replies. Face the conundrum of who to choose. Stalk their profiles to check they're also givers, not just takers. Settle for drawing at random, names from a hat. Amaze at the joy of gifting your stuff. Accept their offerings of home-grown produce, fresh-laid eggs, and immense thanks. Discover that gratitude is priceless.

Finally: Conceding defeat.

Jump out of the shower and don favourite trackpants and hoodie. Pull album at random from teak panelled cabinet. Grin at the cover, Boney M's phat afros and sharp white suits. Slide sleek vinyl from its plastic sleeve. Line up the hole onto the turntable. Raise the arm and blow the needle for dust. Wait through the crackles before swinging shoulders to 'By the Rivers of Babylon'. Lower the drawbridge and select a vintage red. Marvel at the workmanship and the dove-tail joints. Sink into the chesterfield and run a free hand over bumpy buttons. Daydream about a street library for your excess books and planting herbs for an edible verge. Turn your eyes skyward and raise your glass. To quality, longevity, and treading lightly on the Earth.

Cheers: To Dick and Barb.

The Gift of Happiness

William Langrehr

Sera stood in the doorway of her shop, the moon above casting the street in a cold light. The wind blew gently, and the day's heat faded into the night. The stars in the sky twinkled coldly, like gems of ice scattered across the endless void, dangling between existence and oblivion, unsure as to whether they wanted to fall to the earth or drift away.

She produced a jar of dancing lights from a pocket inside her coat; the lights buzzed around the container happily, bumping into the glass walls and off the steel lid. Sera opened the jar and held it towards the sky, allowing the lights to fly away like a cloud of fireflies, humming a quiet melody as they went.

'May you bring happiness,' she whispered, watching them dissipate throughout The Cradle. She smiled softly, closed the door and locked it. She placed the jar on a shelf behind the counter at the back of the store. She opened the trapdoor behind the counter

117

and took a flight of stairs down into her room in the basement, where she remained until the next day.

Sera rose early and unlocked the storefront, propping the door open to allow the summer air to circulate through the rows of antiques, and let the house breathe a little. She then busied herself with dusting the glasses near the front of the store, particularly those near the windows; they seemed to collect ash faster than the others, and she wanted them to really sparkle when the sun started streaming in. She was rearranging some of the jars behind the counter when the stair in front of the door creaked, sending a shiver up her spine. She turned to face her guest and saw a tired-looking man with a shabby cloak and a scraggly beard. Under one arm, he was carrying a crate with a rag over it. The other hung loosely at his side. He offered Sera a small smile, which she returned.

'Welcome to The Wolf's Bane,' Sera recited cheerfully. 'What can I do for you today?'

The man approached and placed his crate on the countertop. 'I've some trinkets to sell. I'm told you're buying,' he explained. 'How much for these?' The man removed the cover, revealing a selection of items, some of which Sera recognised and some she didn't.

Among the trinkets were a collection of small human-looking teeth in a jar, a claw from an ash-strider and, most interestingly, a piece of a shadow. Sera raised her eyebrows and glanced at the man, who was looking through some of the similarly exotic items on Sera's shelves.

'This certainly is quite the assortment you have here. Where did you get all of these, if you don't mind my asking?' she asked.

'The wastes. It's where I work. Boss said I could keep anything I find as part of my pay. Figured I'd try n' get some extra cash for it.'

Sera narrowed her eyes. 'I see,' she said. The man's gaunt expression and laconic speech were beginning to make sense. 'How long have you been working out there? Can't be more than a few weeks, otherwise you would probably not have the legs to be walking with.'

'Oh. I'm a month in. Didn't realise lethality was so high,' the man responded. 'Look, can you pay me or not? I don't mean to be rude, but I'd rather not spend my day off standing around here.'

Sera smiled and looked at the crate again. 'Yes, I understand.' She thought for a moment. 'You shouldn't need money. Waste-workers are always paid well, so what do you need the extra funds for? Saving up for something special?'

'Just don't want this crap piling up in my house. It's one of the few benefits of the job, so may as well capitalise.'

Sera nodded. 'Well, I think I can offer something better than money. If you're willing to try it, I offer a kind of…therapy service. It might help since I know your workplace is quite unpleasant.'

The man frowned. 'Look, I don't have all day. I can't just sit around for an hour and talk.'

Sera shook her head. 'Don't worry. It won't take long at all. I am rather good at it, after all.'

The man pinched the bridge of his nose. 'And what is *it* exactly?'

119

'Nothing too special. I just clean up your mind a little. I can reach in and pluck out a couple of your surface-level emotions. Think of it like…a haircut for your brain. Or like a dentist.'

The man was silent for a while. His eyes seemed to droop, a great weight pressing on them from underneath his eyelids. He swayed on his feet. When he looked at Sera again, he seemed deflated somehow, as though it took all his strength to remain standing.

Sera waved at a door near the back of the store. 'I'll give you a trial. If you're a fan, I'll take these off your hands, and we can consider them paid for. If not, I'll pay you in full. How does that sound?'

The man's shoulders sagged. 'Fine.'

Sera smiled and led him into a small room with a couch and coffee table in the centre. A bench ran along one wall of the room, with a kettle and a selection of teas on top. Sera motioned for the man to sit, closed the door, and took a seat beside him.

'Alright, now close your eyes and give me your hands. This won't take a minute.'

'You said this was going to be like therapy.'

'More so in results than in practice. Now, give me your hands and close your eyes. Though, if you want to hold onto all that negativity, you're free to take payment and go.'

The man thought for a moment. A frown crossed his face, and he went to stand. He paused again, his frown deepening, before he sat back down, and looked at Sera. She gave him a reassuring smile.

The man grumbled, gave Sera his hands, and

closed his eyes.

Sera delved into his mind. She found that he was more deeply wounded than she could heal in a single session. His mind was scarred, and squirmed with the black worms of trauma, drowned in the crimson slime of pain, anchored in memories of loss and suffering. There was nothing she could do to help him, not yet at least. His greatest pains were embedded too deeply to be plucked, too solid to be drained. His mind was mostly closed to her, after all, but she was still able to sort through many of his surface-level emotions, gently collecting those which were causing him the most immediate pain.

She took his sea-urchin-like anxieties and deposited them into a vial where they scratched at the glass, hissed and crackled in the air. The plaque of stress piled up at the bottom of its vial, humming a low bass note. The obsidian chunks of fear clinked into their vial one by one, absorbing each other until one large black crystal sat heavily in its new prison.

She passed over the surface of his mind once more and soothed it where she could. Sera took these emotions, safely separated from the raw flesh of the man's mind and stowed them in a pocket in her jacket. She paused for a moment before running her thumb across the man's forehead.

'Alright, open your eyes. How do you feel?'

'I feel…better, I think. I feel…lighter? How did you…?'

'Oh, the process isn't super interesting. Like I said, it was just a matter of plucking out your negative emotions. The surface-level ones at least. It is not a permanent solution, but it should help you enjoy the rest of the day a little more.'

The man's eyes were brighter and more alert than before. He smiled at Sera, and the smile felt more genuine than the others he had given her. He thanked her, and she led him back to the store. He gave her the crate of items he had brought and bid her farewell. Sera waved goodbye and spent the rest of the day sorting through her new collection.

The majority of her new belongings were distributed throughout the store—organics near the back, minerals in one corner in a large bucket, and scraps of cloth in a small box labelled 'fabrics'.

She brought the most interesting ones to her room underneath the store—the teeth, the scrap of shadow, and the ash-strider's claw. The room was bare, save for a small cupboard standing opposite the ladder, and a brass chandelier which cast a dim orange light. The red walls of the room seemed to gently pulse, thin veins spidering throughout. A few patches of paint were faded and dry, the lights occasionally flickered, and the walls creaked and groaned.

Sera rubbed the faded pink paint and sighed before arranging the vials of emotion and her newly procured items on a shelf in the cupboard. In the low light, she could see that the teeth shimmered, a faint purple lacquer speaking of venomous origins.

'Harvestmen,' she whispered. The lights flickered in response, and Sera scowled. She shook the teeth into her hand and popped one into her mouth. It tasted bitter and acrid, like the smoke of burning hair. This one had clearly been feeding when it died. She spat out the tooth, and tipped the rest on the ground, where the floor immediately grew moist and sticky. The lights in the room flickered for a moment, as the teeth began to smoke before sinking into the floor. As the teeth were consumed, the faded patches of paint regained their full crimson flush, and the room's veins pulsed with renewed vigour.

'May you return what the Harvestmen have taken,' Sera whispered.

Sera was organising a bouquet of orange flowers on her desk. Once she was finished, she propped open the door of The Wolf's Bane and started distributing some fresh acquisitions throughout the store. Just as she finished placing a series of small earthenware jugs on her shelf of homeware goods, she felt a familiar footfall on the front step of the store.

The man had returned, nearly a month after his first visit, carrying a new crate of oddities and wearing the same tired expression he had worn when he first crossed Sera's threshold. Sera gave him a wide, welcoming smile and returned to her desk.

'Welcome back to The Wolf's Bane,' she recited cheerfully.

'Those are nice,' the man said, nodding at the flowers, as he placed his box on the countertop.

Sera smiled at him. 'Thank you. I got them delivered this morning,' she said, before turning her attention to the box's contents. 'Interesting selection today. Though, I was hoping for another scrap of shadow. Or some more Harvestman teeth. How did you get a full jar last time?'

He looked distant and shook his head. 'I don't want to talk about the Harvestmen.' His eyes were bloodshot and teary.

'They've taken a piece of you, haven't they?' Sera said, 'I'm sorry. Those animals are so…tasteless.' She paused, thinking of a way to change the subject. 'What about the shadow? They're usually ambivalent to people like you. What happened there?'

'It was one of the Strangers on the Night Train. They come and go from the fields pretty frequently. Looking for something to eat. They just…left some of themselves behind.'

Sera nodded. 'I see, I see. Well, it's a shame you couldn't get any more. I'm only a few scraps away from a full cloak.'

The man raised an eyebrow. 'Oh? What would someone like you need something like that for?'

Sera smiled. 'Trade secret,' she replied, before looking through the last few items in the box. 'Alright, well, for this, I can probably do you maybe six thousand. How's that sound?'

The man looked at the box, then at Sera, before tapping the countertop with his index finger. He took a breath, exhaled, then went to speak. 'I was actually hoping you could do that therapy thing again. I've had a pretty rough couple of weeks out there.'

'Oh. I'm sorry to hear that. Of course, yes, I can certainly help you. If you want, we can talk about your experiences as well? It can pull some of your unpleasant memories to the forefront so I can trim them off, too. It'll stop you from feeling so bad for a bit longer.'

The man was quiet for a while. 'Will it cost anything extra?' he asked eventually.

'Not at all. Think of it as…a free bonus. Besides, I'm interested in hearing about what you do. I don't get outside these walls that often.'

He nodded. 'There isn't much out there that's worth seeing.'

Sera led the man to the back room, where she brewed him some tea, before taking a seat beside him.

'So, tell me, why work in the wastes? The work pays well, I understand, but surely your suffering can't be paid for so easily.'

The man thought for a while. 'Well…I've not really had much money before. The ash wastes are bad, but The Cradle's worse if you're poor, you know. There's all sorts of trouble waiting out there.' He grimaced. 'I'd have my eyes forfeit if I hadn't taken the job. Though, it's not like living out there is much better than it is here.'

'What exactly do you do out there?'

The man shook his head. 'I maintain mining equipment; the bones of those dead gods are hard, after all, so the kit needs plenty of upkeep. It's dangerous, and thankless too, but I don't envy the miners. They've got it way worse than me. I do thank the spires that I stuck through with my education. Though, the debt's part of the reason I'm out there in the first place.'

'What makes your work so dangerous? If you don't mind my asking.'

'It's the machinery, in part. It never stops, even when we're fixing it. I've seen too many men...friends...taken by those steel jaws. But beyond that, there are these things out there. You know the sort. The ash-striders are always just at the very edge of your vision, still close enough to snatch you away if you're not careful. But there's nothing that can be done about that.' He thought for a second. 'The Strangers on the Night Train, they're harmless, but they stare, their eyeless faces...their teeth. It might not be intentional, but it grates on you like sandpaper. The moon too. It stares at me. Its eyes bleed, and it grins, and it just keeps staring at me.'

Sera placed a reassuring hand on the man's shoulder. He took a deep breath before he continued.

'There's a lot of things, really. But the worst are the—' the man bit off the end of his sentence.

'The Harvestmen?' Sera prompted.

The man shook his head. 'I'm not talking about them. Not today.'

Sera nodded. 'That's okay. I understand.' She offered him her hands. 'Shall we begin?' He took Sera's hands, and the pair closed their eyes.

Sera found the man's mind more open than the last time, and she was free to carefully trim away some of the most hurtful images he had mentioned. She took from him the squid-like grief, which clung to his mind very tightly. She relieved him of his stress and his anxiety. She also took from him some of the memories he had brought to the surface during their talk. Those of his friends' screams as an ash-strider tore him away, and of a new recruit pounding on an airlock as carnivorous dust shredded his bones. Sera scrubbed the black plaque from his mind, leaving it brighter than it had been before. She deposited his memories into one vial, and his emotions into another, stoppering and stowing them in her jacket. The memories scratched at the glass angrily, like trapped spiders.

When the pair opened their eyes, the man was crying, blood running freely down his face. Sera tutted and wiped at the tears with a handkerchief. 'Those Harvestmen did a number on you. You should consider letting me get rid of them next time.'

He sniffed and scrubbed at his eyes, but when he looked at Sera again, he seemed much more at ease. 'Next time…' he whispered. 'Yeah.'

The pair sat for a long while before the man was ready to go again. 'Before I leave,' he said, 'I suppose I should ask your name.'

Sera grinned at him, her golden eyes twinkling. 'My name is Sera. Sera Atrax.'

The man smiled wider than he had before. 'Well, it is a pleasure to make your acquaintance properly, Sera Atrax,' he said, offering her his hand. 'My name is Aren Messor.'

Sera stood at the door of The Wolf's Bane, looking at the night sky. The moon glared out over The Cradle and the wastes beyond—its hollow eyes casting silvered hate wherever it looked. Sera looked at the stars, and reached her hands up, beckoning them down to her. They looked so lost up there, so alone. She wanted to comfort them, to bring them down to her, so she could sit with them. She wanted, too, to be comforted by their light. Perhaps then, neither Sera nor the stars would be so lonely anymore.

Several weeks passed, Aren acting as a welcome disruption to Sera's otherwise uneventful existence. Sometimes, he'd bring her shells from the parasites that clung to the ash-striders' undersides. Sometimes, he'd bring her jars of tiny, swarming clouds of carnivorous dust. He'd even brought her a bag of lost luggage from the Night Train, filled with the rattling and clinking shards of whatever poor soul had decided to rest on the seats too long. Each time, Aren would get Sera to take away his negative emotions and some of his most recent traumatic memories, and Sera would stow them in glass vials.

One day, Aren returned empty-handed save for a bag of coins. There was a dour look on his face and the shadows caught on the edges of his cheeks and pooled in the pits of his eyes. He looked agitated as he approached the counter, placing the money on the bench.

'I need to talk, Sera. I want your advice.'

Sera raised her eyebrows, placing an empty jar on a shelf behind the counter. She waved at the door to the back room. 'Just let yourself in. Hit the kettle, too. I'll be there in a minute.'

When Sera joined him, Aren was sitting on the couch, fiddling with one of the coins from the bag. Two full mugs were sitting on the benchtop, steaming enticingly. Sera handed one to Aren and took a seat beside him.

'What's going on, then, Aren?'

'It's the Harvestmen. They got me yesterday. I was given a week off to recover. I don't think I can anymore, not by myself. They're scurrying around like rats in the gutters of my mind,' Aren spoke quickly, his voice strained.

Sera put a hand on his shoulder, rubbing gently. 'Slowly, Aren. Tell me from the beginning. Just take a deep breath. You're going to be okay.'

Aren exhaled slowly. 'I was walking through one of the ventilation tunnels. Had to make sure the dark wasn't starting to coagulate. Blocks airflow, see. But they…the Harvestmen, they were waiting for me. The first one crawled down the wall in front of me, like a damn spider.' Aren took a shaky breath. 'It looked like us, you know? Just…wrong. Malformed, like its bones were all broken and healed incorrectly.'

Aren was quiet for a moment, his eyes closed, his brow furrowed in pain. 'It just watched me. Its eyes were the worst. Golden like yours but sunk deep into its face. It laughed. Giggled, like a child…

'I turned to try and run, but there were more behind me, three of them. They looked identical. Grey skin and all. I could tell they were excited; they just grinned at me. They knew I couldn't get out.

'They pinned me down. Held my arms and legs,

stretched me thin. Their fingers wriggled their way into my protective suit, and they just…stole chunks of me. And they *laughed.* They just *laughed* at me.

'It's all I could hear as they left. I couldn't see. I couldn't breathe. I couldn't hear anything but their damn laughs. I was screaming, I think, until my throat bled. I felt like I needed to pull my skin off.'

Aren turned his hands over to reveal purple, twisted fingers. 'They broke my hands…they broke my feet. I couldn't…'

Aren took a deep breath and choked down a sob. 'Another maintenance crew came through and found me three days later. I was sure I was going to die out there. My boss gave me a dose of quick-set for my hands and feet, and told me to be back next week…I just…I can't…I…'

Sera put Aren's mug on the table as he began to sob, before wrapping him in a tight hug. The two of them closed their eyes, and Sera dove into his mind. She took many of the deeper memories this time, carving away anything that could give him pain, any memory associated with the Harvestmen. She pulled many of the worms of trauma from his mind and drained nearly all of the red gel of pain. She deposited it all into a series of jars; the vials she had used previously were far too small to fit them all.

She went back over his mind, and though it felt smaller, it was free from all the suffering that had plagued him for so long. She soothed the sore wounds, and softened the pain of the surgery, before gently kissing him on the forehead, and drawing him out of his stupor. She put the jars into her jacket before Aren opened his eyes, which were clear and alert, more so than they had been before.

'How are you feeling, Aren?' Sera asked softly.

'Good. Yeah, I'm feeling really good. Better than I have in ages. Thank you, Sera, thank you so much. Here's your pay. Thank you.'

Sera smiled kindly. 'Now, what was that advice you needed from me?'

'Oh yeah. Sera, do you think I should quit my job?'

Sera thought for a moment, her smile widened, and she spoke. 'No, I don't think so. Why would you ever want to quit your job?'

Aren frowned and hesitated. 'You know what, I don't remember.'

Sera smiled at Aren and took the coins from him before handing him his mug of tea. Eventually, Aren left again, allowing Sera to stow the money in her safe and put away the memories in her room. The crimson walls seemed to glow, the veins pulsing powerfully, fed by the months of trinkets that Aren had been providing. Sera sorted through the vials and jars of memories and emotion, slurping down the writhing worms of trauma, relishing in the way they thrashed in her throat.

She let out a satisfied sigh. 'May you never again bring harm.'

Sera looked over some of the memories she had harvested from Aren, her nose wrinkling in disgust when she came to the memories of the Harvestmen. She had no use for them, so she placed the sealed jar on the floor of her room, and watched as the memories struggled, died, and were burned away.

'Filthy creatures, ruining everything they touch. They really have no class.'

A week later, Aren returned to The Wolf's Bane, looking worse than ever. Sera offered him the same smile she always had. Aren was a wreck, pale-faced and shaking, barely able to walk in a straight line. Sera went to him and helped him into the back room, lowering him gently onto the couch.

'Deep breaths now, Aren. Deep breaths now. That's good. Tell me what's wrong.'

'I…I went back to work, like normal, but there were all these…these *things* out there. People are *dying*, Sera, and nobody seems to care! My boss said I was having an *episode*…told me to come back when I felt better.'

Sera embraced Aren, stroking the back of his head soothingly.

'It's okay, it's alright,' she said. 'Deep breaths now, I've got you.'

Aren sobbed into Sera's chest, his arms wrapped tightly, desperately, around her, as she gently whispered to him, a small smile spreading across her face. Eventually, Aren's breathing stabilised, and the sobbing gave way to the occasional sniffle. He looked into Sera's eyes, bloody tears running down his face.

'Everything hurts,' he said. 'Everything hurts so much, Sera.'

She gently kissed his forehead. 'I can help you, Aren. Because you're my friend, I can help you. But you'll need to trust me. I can make all the hurt go away, but you'll need to open your mind to me. More than ever before.'

Aren nodded, his eyes downcast. 'Please. Just make it stop. Make it all stop.'

Sera smiled at him and stood, helping him to his feet. 'Alright. I'll do it free of charge this time since we're such good friends. Just follow me. It'll all be over soon. You'll be happy, I promise.'

Sera led Aren back into the store and down the stairs to her room, taking one of the jars from the shelves behind the counter with her.

'There's no bed in here,' Aren said. 'Where do you sleep?'

Sera smiled at him sweetly. 'I don't. But don't worry about me. We're here for you. Just lie on the floor over there. I'll be right with you.'

'What are those jars, Sera? What's going on?'

Sera turned to Aren and put her hand on his cheek, gently rubbing it with her thumb. 'Trust me, Aren. You need to be calm. You'll be alright. Now go lie down on the floor, please.'

Aren nodded again and did as Sera asked.

She prepared a selection of jars, looking over the now-empty vials that used to contain Aren's negative emotions. She arranged them beside Aren and sat cross-legged behind him.

'They're just to hold your pain, Aren. Don't want

them getting out and hurting anyone else.'

Aren shook his head. 'Sera, why does the floor feel so sticky?'

'It's nothing to worry about. Just give me your hand; we'll be done here soon, and you can go back outside.'

Aren closed his eyes and Sera took his hand. His mind was open to her in its entirety, and she began trimming all the negative emotions she could find. Then she moved onto the memories. She took them all, leaving only the happy ones. She deposited them into one of the large jars and sealed his emotions in vials. She then started working on the pain, separating his mind from his body so he couldn't feel his old injuries anymore. Sera continued severing Aren's now blissful mind from his body, trimming away one connection at a time, ensuring that he couldn't feel a thing.

When she was done, all that was left of Aren were happy memories, which Sera placed in a final jar. Sera stood and stretched, cracking her neck, and put the jars full of negativity and memory on her shelf. Below, Aren's body began to smoke, the house's walls pulsing harder and faster, its veins flaring, as it digested the inert human remains.

Sera downed one of the vials of negative emotion to restore her energy and returned upstairs. In her hand, she held the jar containing the brilliantly glowing embers of Aren's now blissful mind.

That night, Sera stood in the doorway of her shop, the moon above her casting the street in a cold light. The wind blew gently, and the day's heat faded into the night. The stars above her twinkled coldly, like gems of ice scattered across the endless void, dangling between existence and oblivion, unsure as to whether they wanted to fall to earth or drift away.

She produced a jar full of dancing lights from a pocket inside her coat; the lights buzzed around the container happily. Sera opened the jar and held it towards the sky, allowing the lights to fly away like a cloud of fireflies, humming a quiet melody as they went.

'May you bring happiness,' she whispered, watching them disappear into the night. She smiled softly and closed the door.

Wolfe's Antiques

The Path to the Dream

Elena Sopotsko

A chilly fog drifted over the small Norse town, between dark, gloomy houses barely visible through the muddy shroud of night, until it dissolved into the forest, from which the haunting cry of the wolves echoed. This doleful howl started quietly, then grew louder, filling everything around until it penetrated through the dense fog, reaching every corner of the town. On the edge of town, a light appeared in one of the buildings, illuminating a faded sign on the door reading 'Wolfe's Antiques'. Starting quietly first and then growing stronger, this howl seemed to occupy the entire space.

Old Wolfe, who lived at the back of his shop, slid heavily off the bed, rubbed his sleepy, watery eyes with his fists, and threw a moth-eaten woollen sweater over his shoulders. Ever since he was young, he would wake up to the howling, go to the window, and peer into the darkness. He would wait until his covert guests, exhausted after a sleepless night, gathered in his basement to rest.

And now, here they came. Old and young. Their skin was scratched, blood dripped from their mouths, and their knees were smeared with dirt. Growling, they ran on all fours down the stairs and disappeared into his basement's labyrinth.

Wolfe called himself The Keeper, although perhaps it was too solemn a title, because the only things he possessed were secrets.

All her life, Nora had had dreams about the wolves. Most often, she dreamt of a giant, black wolf with a radiant white halo around its head, The Great Wolf. He revealed to her how the passages to other worlds unfolded, where mermaids, trolls, and elves dwelled. The dreams of wolves were the most vivid events in Nora's life. They whisked Nora away to a realm of enchantment and mysteries. She hoped that one day something might happen that would allow her to see such a life not only in a dream. In reality, her life was completely different—cosy and homely.

Nineteen-year-old Nora had a casual job in a local store. She lived with her mother, Ann, a schoolteacher, in a small town, where time seemed to stand still; its rhythm lost in the ancient echo of Norse legends and the wild spirit of the forest that bordered it. The occasional glow of a phone screen or the hum of a car engine served as the only reminders that the world beyond had marched on into a new era, barely touching the timeless existence of the town's inhabitants.

That evening, after their traditional tea with homemade cake, Nora and Ann sat down to watch a movie, nestled under a large, cosy throw. This is how their evenings had passed since Nora's childhood. Nora's father had died when she was a year old, and Ann had decided to devote her life to her daughter.

Later, Nora entered her bedroom and went to the window. The thin crescent moon shone above the town. Mournful wolves' howls came from the forest. Sinister rumours had long circulated about the woods surrounding the town. It was said that werewolves lived there and preyed on people; the one who ruled over these werewolves was a wolf with human eyes. With those eyes, he seared the souls of people, transforming them into wolves. Nora sat beside her window for the best part of the night, listening to the wolves' howling. She eventually fell asleep with her cheek pressed against the window. She smiled in her sleep, dreaming of The Great Wolf. He turned his back to Nora and sauntered off. Nora followed him. They walked through the town, where everything was tangible and bright, as if in reality. The Great Wolf led Nora to the edge of the town where the forest began. He went to a building, which displayed a sign reading, 'Wolfe's Antiques', and disappeared.

In the morning, Nora awoke, determined to visit the mysterious shop. She navigated her way through the narrow streets of the town, her steps echoing against the cobblestone pathways. Although she had walked this route countless times before, today it felt as though each turn was leading her directly to a destination she had passed many times before but never truly noticed. The shop now stood out to her, although its small sign on the door was faded and almost unreadable. Under the sign was a door knocker in the shape of a wolf's head.

As she entered, the shop enveloped her in its dim, hushed ambience. There was the scent of aged wood, dust, and the faint fragrance of old paper. Behind the counter, an elderly man in a woollen sweater was reading a weathered book. Nora meandered through the narrow aisles, her fingers lightly grazing the spines of ageing tomes, until she stood before an antique mirror.

She met her own glittering, amber eyes in the reflection but, to her astonishment, Nora noticed a second pair of amber eyes gazing at her. Looking closer, she saw a portrait of The Great Wolf behind her. Nora whirled around and an unsettling shiver coursed down her spine. Instead of The Great Wolf's portrait, there was a framed depiction of a saint; an icon painted with intricate detail, hung on the wall. Casting another glance at the mirror, Nora again was met by the gaze of The Great Wolf.

The old man appeared beside her. She hadn't noticed him approaching.

'What's wrong with this portrait?' Nora asked.

'What are you talking about?' The old man frowned, looking carefully at her with his reddened, watery eyes.

'In the reflection I see a wolf instead of this saint.'

'It's called the Hell Icon,' the man said. 'Artists paint The Devil, or a pagan god, and depict a Christian saint on top. This unique form of art relies on a sophisticated layering technique,' he continued, his voice a blend of reverence and mystery. 'Beneath the serene visage of the saint, the artist carefully integrates another image using materials that respond differently to light and shadow. To most, the dominant image of the saint is all that's visible. However, to those sensitive to the energies and the subtleties of this art, the underlying figure can reveal itself. It's not just about the physical eyesight; it's about the perception of the soul. The fact that you see The Wolf indicates a rare connection to the deeper, often hidden energies of these icons. It's a manifestation of the duality within—the visible and the invisible, the saintly and the wild—coexisting in harmony. Some people can feel the energy from the hidden image. You are the first visitor to see The Wolf.'

'Could you tell me about this wolf?'

'Not now,' the old man replied. 'Don't tell anyone about this icon. What is your name?'

'Nora. When will you tell me?'

'Come tomorrow evening. My name is Argus Wolfe. Nice to meet you, Nora.'

From his earliest memories, Argus, like all children in the town, knew that the forest was a place of danger, a lesson reinforced by his father's stern warnings.

'As soon as the sun sets, steer clear of the forest. They reside in our vicinity,' his father would often say, his voice carrying the weight of unspoken fear.

Argus had pestered his father, 'Who are they?', but his father did not answer. He was withdrawn and silent, always confined to his antique shop, only leaving on business. Sometimes, he was absent for several days, which shrouded him in an aura of mystery.

The only thing that made his father happy was something he kept hidden in a wooden chest. One day, while his father was away, Argus found the key and opened the chest. There was an icon depicting a saint. He disappointedly put it back, but then felt amber eyes peering at him through the saint's image. The longer he looked, the more clearly the face of The Wolf appeared. Frightened, Argus had slammed the lid of the chest.

When Argus turned eighteen, his father told him that the Wolfe family were hereditary keepers of the mystery of The Great Wolf. Argus took an oath never to tell anyone about this, never to try to become one of them, and most importantly, to promise to keep the icon forever. From that evening, his father taught Argus about the sacred rites associated with the icon, about the wolf people, and how to become a wolf.

A year later, his father gave him the icon and said, 'Keep it, as I have kept it throughout my life. The day will come when this icon brings different people into your life. And then you, son, will teach them everything I taught you.'

Argus was stunned into silence. That night, his father had left home, and Argus became the Keeper. Argus never married; he was unsociable and lived in a small room in his antique shop.

Various people came to the shop, and those who stood in front of the icon for a long time, Argus invited to his basement—the place where his Pack gathered.

The following evening, once her workday had concluded, Nora came back to Wolfe's shop.

Argus greeted her with a warm smile, beckoning her to a discreet side door that opened to a concealed staircase. Together, they descended, traversing a winding, labyrinthine corridor that eventually led to a spacious chamber. Within, people were seated comfortably on bean bags, and an imposing painting of The Great Wolf adorned one of the walls.

'Nora heard The Great Wolf's call,' Argus announced. 'I invited her to be your sister.'

The room's occupants regarded her with a mix of caution and curiosity. An aged woman broke the silence.

'What do you know about The Wolf?' she inquired.

'He comes to me in my dreams,' Nora answered. 'He showed me this store. But I don't know anything about him. Who is he?'

'The Great Wolf is neither human nor animal; he is an ancient god,' Argus said, pointing to the large portrait. 'These people are his blood brothers and sisters, the wolf people. In every country, there are legends about them. People call them werewolves. Anyone who hears The Great Wolf's call can become a werewolf,' Argus continued, 'but only a few dare to undergo the initiation. We help those summoned to awaken the wolf blood in themselves and prepare for the initiation. You are all of one blood, Nora. Welcome to the Pack.'

Nora couldn't believe it; she was surrounded by seemingly ordinary people.

'Chris.' Argus turned to a young woman. 'You will help Nora.'

Chris came over and smiled. 'We'll need to keep in touch; let's exchange numbers. I'll teach you how to awaken the wolf in you today.'

'Today?' Nora was surprised.

'Why not?' Chris shrugged. 'Let's go.'

'What does it mean to awaken the wolf in me?' Nora asked once they were outside.

'At first, you have to feel what the wolves feel. Become a part of the forest, throw all thoughts away, and feel the Call of the Moon.' Chris pulled Nora into the woods.

'Are we...going into the forest? In the dark?' Nora's voice quivered with trepidation, her wide eyes betraying her fear. Chris smiled.

'Get used to it,' she said. 'We are special.'

Chris led Nora into the clearing and got down on all fours.

'All you must do is stand on all fours and try to feel that you are a wolf, an ancient creature, a part of a huge world. You can howl quietly. It's like meditation. Try it.'

Nora hesitantly got down on all fours, trying not

to stain her jeans. It all seemed like a silly prank. She'd expected something extraordinary. But this... She felt like an idiot.

'Listen, Chris...' she paused, speechless.

Chris' limbs lengthened, turning into paws. Fur grew through her skin. The young woman's face lengthened, turning into an animal muzzle. Chris let out a chilling howl, and with powerful leaps, darted deep into the forest. Nora's heart leapt in her chest, and a startled cry escaped her lips. Left alone in the nocturnal forest, she rose to her feet and, shuddering at every rustle, hurried home, cursing herself for her ill-fated curiosity.

Over evening tea, Nora told her mother that she had met a new friend, Chris, without mentioning the details of the meeting.

That night, The Great Wolf haunted Nora's dream again, its fury palpable as it bared its teeth. Wrath blazed in its eyes. In the morning, Nora was woken by her phone ringing.

'So, you thought it was too strange and ran away?' Chris' cheerful voice came through the phone. 'We've all been there. Give it another try, perhaps in the daylight. Just bring a yoga mat. If anyone spots you, they'll think you're practising yoga.'

Nora pondered it. The nightmare had scared her, and she decided to go to the forest, just to prove it was not for her. She dressed in a tracksuit, picked up her yoga mat and headed for the forest.

Unrolling the mat in the forest clearing, she got on all fours. Initially, she couldn't shake the feeling of foolishness and peculiarity, but eventually, her anxieties melted away. From this position, the forest looked different. It seemed to wrap itself around her. She watched the grass sway in the wind and listened to the rustle of the trees and the chirping of the birds. Suddenly, it was as if a string had snapped inside her. Tears streamed down her face. She began swaying gently and feeling the essence of the forest filling her.

From then on, she went to the forest every day after work, trying to arrive on time for evening tea with her mother afterwards. It was still a sacred time, where the day's events were shared and discussed over cups of warm tea, reinforcing the threads of connection and understanding that had always united them.

On the night of the full moon, Chris said, 'On the full and new moons, we join our older brothers and sisters, the Great Wolf Pack. Some of them used to be werewolves, too.' She turned to Nora. 'Today is a big day for you. You will become a werewolf.'

'What if I can't?' Nora became worried. She had dreamed about this ever since she met the Pack.

'You can,' Chris assured her. 'Call home. Tell your mother you're staying with me for the night. You will turn into a human again at dawn.'

When they entered the forest, the moon shone brightly. She felt her heartbeat in her throat.

'For the first time, it'll be painful and take about an hour,' Chris said. 'Get on all fours, awaken the wolf in you and without stopping, look at the moon. Be patient and wait.'

Nora raised her head to the sky. The moonlight was popping in front of her eyes, and she felt sick and giddy. Abruptly, an immense pain pierced Nora. Still looking at the moon, she fell to the ground and began shaking in agony. Her skin burned like fire, and her body twisted unnaturally as bones reshaped. It seemed to Nora that several hours had passed when, finally, the pain subsided, and she saw fur growing from her body. Chris smiled at her, got down on all fours, transformed into a wolf, and disappeared into the bushes.

Nora was filled with an unprecedented delight. She rushed into the forest, feeling the branches cracking under her strong paws as the wind ruffled the fur on her back.

Nora was scouring the forest, sniffing the ground for prey, when the smell of blood attracted her. At the path's edge lay a wounded bird. Nora approached and licked it. The flesh was slightly salty and warm. Nora dug her teeth into the bird, cracking thin bones and spitting out feathers. Having sated her hunger, she moved quietly along the path, her ears tuned to the night forest's sounds. All her senses were sharpened. She reached the creek, quenched her thirst, and began to howl, looking at the moon's reflection in the black water. She gave herself entirely to this sound, dissolving in it. All her human thoughts, problems and doubts disappeared, and only this long, melancholic song remained, bringing her a happiness she had never experienced before.

At dawn, a sharp pain pierced Nora's body. She lay down on the ground and waited. The worst part was that, along with her wolf form, her vitality was leaving her. The world seemed to dim; colours, sounds, and scents grew dull, and her energy vanished. Struggling to her feet, she slowly made her way back home.

The happiness of freedom consumed Nora. All she wanted was to feel her teeth digging into soft living flesh and, most importantly, to sense that euphoria of merging with the world again and again.

Nora desperately wanted to share the happiness of her new life with her mother. One day, over a cup of tea, she said, 'Mum, would you like to see the forest at night?'

'Are you kidding me? There are wolves there,' Ann laughed.

'Maybe these are werewolves, not wolves. Werewolves are people like us.'

'No,' Anne said. 'Werewolves are beasts. There is nothing human about them. They can bite their loved ones to death and not feel remorse about it.'

'Mum, they are ordinary people. They won't kill anyone.'

'They are not people,' Ann whispered, lips trembling, and left the room.

Summer passed, and Nora continued to escape into the woods every evening. On a gloomy autumn day, she went to Argus.

'I want to go through the Initiation,' she said. 'Being half-wolf, half-human is like being half-dead and half-alive. I want to live a full life.'

Argus smiled. He had been waiting for such a person for many years. His service to The Great Wolf was to find someone ready to throw off human bonds and go free. His Pack—they had all heard the Call and became werewolves, but still, there was more human in them than animal. He watched them when they gathered in his basement after a hunt. Half-people, half-beasts. It was as if they were playing werewolves, afraid or not daring to go further. But Nora…

'Do you know how your father died?' he asked.

She shook her head.

'He was a werewolf too, and he also wanted to undergo the Initiation. This Ritual…it's not for everyone. You will not be able to change your mind. You'll either lose your human qualities and become a wolf or…'

'Or?' Nora asked.

'Or you will die a terrible death like your father.'

'I'm ready,' Nora whispered, turning pale. 'Tell me about the Ritual.'

Argus looked at her.

'Well, first you must discard all human feelings and emotions, including attachment to people, things, or life. This is the most challenging part. Once you've accomplished that, you must venture into the forest on the night of the new moon. Take off your clothes, go into the clearing, and call the wolves. They will come, and you must say, "Oh Wolves, eat the human; leave the wolf." If you are truly ready for the Ritual, the Wolves will not harm you, and you will emerge as a She-Wolf. Your soul will be reborn; you'll no longer be able to turn into a human, but you'll find a happiness you never dreamed of. If even a shadow of love or regret flashes through you, the wolves will tear you to pieces, and that's a terrible death, Nora. Think before you decide.'

She nodded and left.

Nora walked around the town, torn by her decision. The thought of leaving her mother alone weighed heavily on her heart. How would Ann cope with the loss of her daughter? Nora came to a sudden stop, emotions overwhelming her. She called Chris.

'Chris, have you ever thought about the Ritual?'

'No. The Ritual is sacrifice. You sacrifice either your life or the lives of your loved ones. Think about your mother; your decision will kill her.' Chris paused. 'You know, Argus is my uncle. His parents loved each other, but his father underwent the Ritual and became a wolf. His mother hanged herself; she couldn't live without him.'

'I will think.' Nora lowered her head.

Returning home, Nora saw her mother waiting for her.

'I baked some cookies,' Ann said, her eyes filled with love and concern. 'Let's have some tea.'

Nora cried, hugging her mum.

'There, there, sunshine,' Ann said, kissing Nora. 'Everything will be fine. Don't you cry.'

'I love you, Mum,' Nora whispered.

Having resigned herself to the idea that the Ritual

wasn't meant for her, Nora stopped running into the forest and meeting Chris. She spent her evenings with Ann, read, watched movies, and cried at night.

A week later, in the evening, Nora was washing dishes when a glass burst in her hands, cutting her finger. She automatically put her finger in her mouth, and the taste of the fresh blood, like an explosion, awakened in her everything she had tried to suppress.

Ann heard the door slam, looked out the window, and saw Nora near the forest. As if in slow motion, she watched her daughter disappearing among the dark trees. Ann's blood ran cold. She knew what this meant. Her husband had also ventured into the woods during the evenings. Ann remembered how one day, having returned dirty and exhausted, he had brought a dog chain and begged her to tie him to the bed so that he could not leave the home. She refused, thinking it was too much. He left that night, and the next morning, people found his torn body at the edge of the forest. Fear for Nora's safety forced Ann to act. She got the old dog chain from the shed and waited for Nora to come back.

Nora returned by morning, dirty and half-dead from exhaustion, and went straight to her bedroom. Ann followed her in.

'I saw you in the woods,' Ann started.

Nora, without responding, laid down in bed.

'I'm worried about you, sweetheart,' Ann continued.

'I'm okay, Mum. Let's talk tomorrow,' Nora mumbled as she drifted asleep.

Ann approached her daughter. Her hands were covered in dirt and dried blood was on her face. Crying, Ann locked the chain on the iron bars of the massive bed and with the other end of the chain, locked Nora's ankle. She locked the shutters on the windows and left the room.

In the morning, Ann woke up to furious screams. She sighed, then called Nora's boss and said her daughter was sick.

At the end of autumn, Chris met Argus and inquired how long it had been since he'd seen Nora.

'She's been missing for about a month now. I called her, but she didn't answer,' Chris explained. 'I went to her place, but her mother wouldn't let me in. She said Nora was sick. I think something's wrong.'

'I'll go see her. Wait for me here.' Argus' brows furrowed, etching deep lines of concern into his face.

He came to Nora's house in the evening and knocked. There was no answer. One of the windows facing the side was covered with shutters. He shook his head. The door was unlocked, and he entered.

'Ann? Nora?' he called. The house was quiet. Argus walked through the house, looking into every room. He approached a closed door. A small key hung on a nail driven into a door jamb. Argus put the key into his pocket, slowly opened the door, and immediately met Nora's direct, intense stare.

She stood on all fours, her shoulders tense, every vein visible on her bare arms. Her head was bent to the ground like a dog ready to attack, and a reddish stream of saliva hung from her chapped lips. When he entered, Nora, without taking her eyes off him, lifted her upper lip, revealing yellowed teeth. Argus took a step forward, and a warning growl escaped her lips.

The room smelled heavily of unwashed body, blood, and excrement. At the door, in a pool of half-dried blood, lay the corpse of a woman with her throat torn out. Nearby was a plate of dried porridge, which had not been touched. Argus carefully walked around the corpse and spoke.

'Nora, I came to let you go,' he said imperiously. 'Let me come over and take off the chain.'

Nora tilted her head. A hint of realisation flashed in her gaze for a moment, and then she bared her teeth and growled. Argus was confused, feeling her fierce, ancient, blood-hungry hatred. However, he managed to pull himself together quickly. He slowly approached the young woman and, with her fetid breath on his face, inserted the key into the lock.

Feeling freedom, Nora jumped out of the house and rushed towards the forest. Argus returned to his store and asked Chris to call the police.

Two days later, Ann's funeral brought together all the townspeople, except Nora. After the funeral, Chris came to Argus.

'Why?' she cried. 'Why do people, striving for their

goal, forget about their loved ones? How could she do this to Ann?'

'A great goal always requires sacrifice, my dear. The higher the goal, the higher the price. If Ann had won, then Nora's life would have been sacrificed. So wags the world, Chris.'

'But when I'm a werewolf, my goals are completely different. Oh god, what if someday I too... No. Never! I don't want to be a werewolf anymore,' Chris said firmly, looking at him with eyes swollen from tears.

Argus sighed, rummaged around his desk, and pulled out a small, round box. He handed it to her, saying, 'This night, you will strip naked and rub this ointment all over your face and your body. After that, you'll go to the icon of The Great Wolf in my basement and, looking into his eyes, shout, "I renounce!" Understood?'

Chris nodded, took the ointment, and hugged Argus.

On the night of the full moon, a clear, low, and confident wolf's howl came from the forest. Argus knew it was Nora. He was sure that tonight Nora had turned into a She-Wolf. He locked his shop and entered the forest.

Argus stood among the trees, peering into the impenetrable darkness. A She-Wolf appeared beside him. She was larger than a regular wolf; her fur was black, and a white glow emanated from her. She looked at Argus with Nora's amber eyes, licked his hand and disappeared into the darkness of the night. Argus smiled and headed back to his store.

Nora howled. Other wolves echoed her from all sides of the forest and the air was filled with the anticipation of something special, as if some vital milestone had been passed. The wolves were gathering on the top of the hill. It was their moon, their night, and their She-Wolf.

Argus stood at the window, pressing his forehead against the dirty glass and listening to the dismal howl. Through the fog of his memory, he saw the shadows of lives sacrificed, relationships lost, and the dim faces of those who went in search of their dreams, leaving emptiness and secrets behind. The secrets he kept.

Her Sister's Song

Holly Letcher

All is still in Dr Wolfe's House of Whimsical Wonders, but for the ticking of the great-great-grandfather clock and the padding of socked feet across the floor of the apartment above. A plank groans in annoyance at a slight misjudgement of weight. A girl's face peers back to an open bedroom door. She listens for signs of Mum stirring. Nothing. She continues down the stairs, extra vigilant this time.

She wades through countless aisles of shelves that carry the weight of the world on their planks, holding treasures and artefacts from across the entire globe, and further still. There are whistles that seem to play themselves, dolls whose lacy skirts sit slightly differently each morning, and empty teapots which look as though they'd still be warm. She passes under the chandeliers that never lose their shine, past the paintings that don't look quite like they did yesterday, and to the corner, where the shelves are laden with books. She spots her target and grabs a small, wooden stool. Mum thought she didn't see where she'd hidden it…or perhaps that she wouldn't be able to reach.

She huffs as she stretches her arm, fingers barely brushing the edge of the leather spine. She rises to her tiptoes. *Got it!* The stool wobbles. *Uh oh.* She clings to the shelf as the stool clatters over. After deciding it's safe, she lets go and lands on the wooden floor with a soft thud. She pats the shelf and whispers a friendly thanks.

Clutching her book, she weaves around the maze of trinkets and goods and through the intense curtains that lead to the rooms at the back of the shop.

An upright piano with warm wood and a gentle demeanour sits against the wall. The instrument almost ripples with magic as she lifts the fallboard. She opens the book and flicks through pages of music, until she finds what she is after—'An Elegy for Lost Ones'. She lays the book across the music desk. Foot firmly planted on the mute pedal, she positions her fingers for the first chord and starts to play.

Each note that looks oppositional on the page comes together, forming a tune that is discordant, yet pleasant. It doesn't matter that her fingers are clumsy or that the sound stops whenever she has to rearrange her hands. Every accent, arpeggio, and crescendo is a cacophony of laughs, tears, and hugs. It sounds like a home she remembers but hasn't seen in a long time.

'Charlotte?'

The music stops. Charlotte looks behind her to where her sister stands, staring at her, confused.

Charlotte sucks in a breath and holds onto it. It

certainly looks like Kiara—same freckles, same knowing eyes, same faded scar above her lip from where Mr Whiskers played too rough. It almost looks as though the light passes through her.

Charlotte shuffles off the piano stool. Before she can tell it not to, her hand reaches out to hold Kiara's. It's soft, but reassuringly solid. She squeezes it. Kiara squeezes back.

Charlotte embraces her sister, burying her face into her shoulder. Kiara's arms tighten across her back, her chin resting on Charlotte's head. Charlotte scrunches her eyes so the tears have nowhere to go.

'Ladybug,' Kiara whispers, her fingers slowly weaving through Charlotte's hair, 'why am I here?'

Charlotte focuses on her sister's breathing. She remembers it being reliable and soothing. Now, it feels…hollow.

'I want more time.'

Charlotte waits for the telling off that she is bound to get, but Kiara just keeps stroking her hair and holding her tight. That's good. Were she to let go, Charlotte may very well fall apart.

A mother sits at a piano, constructing a jolly tune. A daughter dances clumsily about the room, weaving around the butterflies floating through the air. A father dances with her, twirling the young girl under his arm. A smaller daughter sits at the piano beside the mother, watching her fast-moving fingers, a content smile on her lips.

Charlotte wakes up on the floor, alone, when the sun has trickled through the whole shop and landed just below the edge of the keyhole on the piano. A familiar emptiness hits her in the chest, leaving her grasping for breath.

She thought last night would get rid of this feeling. Apparently not.

After listening for any sounds of Mum and deciding there are none, Charlotte half-tiptoes, half-runs through the aisles, up the stairs, and into her room, remembering to replace the music book on the way. She closes the door, slides back into bed and, for the rest of the morning, watches the empty side of her room.

The room was supposed to get smaller as she got bigger. Yet, here she is with more space than she could ever get used to.

Charlotte lies in her bed, trying to remember how to breathe.

'Mr Whiskers, how on earth did you get up there?'

Mum plucks the stuffed cat from the top of the bookshelf. 'You must have had quite the adventure last night,' she tells it.

Charlotte rolls her eyes as she collects the teacups laid out on the floor. The shop is always messier in the morning than it is at night, but Charlotte can't understand why Mum insists on talking to the toys during the day—it's not like they can hear her.

Charlotte steps over the circle of dead-eyed dolls, under the dusty chandelier, and past the faded paintings, to put the teacups back in their place by the chipped teapot. When she surveys the shelves to find anything else out of place, she spots the piano peeking through a gap in the curtains.

'Mum?'

'Mhmm?'

'Can I play the piano?'

'Go for it.'

'No, I mean,' Charlotte falters, staring at the curtains, 'can I play it tonight?'

Mum comes around a shelf, dusting her hands on her apron, and gives Charlotte a serious look.

'I think you know the answer to that.'

'But it's only fun when the sun's down!'

'Yes.' Mum places her hands on her hips and plasters on a calm smile. 'And you become a grumpy bear when you don't get enough sleep.'

She's doing that thing adults do when they think kids are too young to understand the real reason.

'The sun goes down a bit before bedtime. Can't I play it then?' she tries.

'No.'

'Why not?' This time, Charlotte doesn't even try to hide the whinge in her voice. Mum responds with a look icy enough to stop a pair of eyes mid-roll.

'Because I said so.'

Charlotte scowls at the floor. Mum brushes it off and walks away. 'I'm sorry, but I'm not changing my mind.' She flips the sign on the front door to 'open'. Charlotte huffs.

'That's not what sorry means,' she mutters, stomping down the aisle.

Charlotte sneaks down the stairs, quicker than last night. The day passed so slowly. It took a year for the sun to set, and then a whole decade for Mum to fall asleep.

Charlotte retrieves the music book from the high shelf, this time noting its *exact* position. She can't be too careful, not after seeing Mum inspecting that very shelf earlier that day.

She sits at the piano, steps on the mute pedal, and plays.

She's not any better than she was last night, but it still doesn't matter. That's the magic of magic; it makes even the most ordinary things wonderful.

This time, Charlotte notices Kiara's arrival instantly. She immediately runs to her for a hug.

'You brought me here again.'

'Please.' Charlotte squeezes tighter. 'I need more time.'

'Does Mum know you're down here?'

Charlotte freezes, accidentally confirming her guilt.

'Charlotte—'

'What does it matter if she said no? This is more important.'

Kiara regards her with something between disappointment and worry. She takes an empty breath.

'Alright. But this has to be the last night,' Kiara says. Charlotte avoids her stern look. 'Charlotte, I'm serious. I need you to promise me.'

Charlotte frowns and grumbles a reluctant promise. She's not entirely sure her sister doesn't see her fingers crossing behind her back, but Kiara doesn't say anything.

Tonight, Charlotte suggests they play the piano together—the song that Mum or Dad used to play for them, the one with the butterflies. But Kiara says no; playing another song would make her disappear. They can't close the fallboard, and Kiara can't leave the back room either.

'But why?' Charlotte asks.

'Because magic is fragile,' Kiara explains. 'And I'm not *really* here. You know that, don't you?'

She does. She'd just managed to convince herself out of it.

So, to pass the time, Charlotte finds a few books that they used to love from the kids' section. They steal the cushion from the piano stool to put on the floor and find blankets in a nearby basket to wrap themselves in. Kiara hugs Charlotte close to her as she reads. She even does the funny voices, just like she used to.

For a moment, Charlotte can forget that Kiara doesn't have a shadow.

Soon, Charlotte's eyelids become heavy. Though she tries desperately to fight off sleep, she can't stop the edges of reality from starting to blur.

'You're alright, Ladybug. You're alright,' a daughter whispers to her younger sister, wrapping her in a warm embrace, showing her how to breathe again. The younger sister calms. A mother sits in a plastic chair beside them, so far away that her children can barely see her. A constant trickle of people move past them, some wearing scrubs, some wheeling carts or beds, some waiting as anxiously as them. But the one man they want to see is hidden from them by a series of walls, protocols, and anaesthetic.

'You're alright, Ladybug. You're alright.'

Charlotte's eyes flutter open. She spots the sunlight at the edge of the curtain. How did that happen? How could she let herself fall asleep? Charlotte leans into Kiara and tries to copy her breaths, but all she can do is imagine what it is like when they are gone. Kiara seems to notice something is wrong, but she just keeps reading. And that's good. But when the sunlight finally touches the foot of the piano, Charlotte's arms are empty once more. She slumps onto the hard floor,

168

gasping for air.

She stays there for a long time, long after she regains her breath, and long after she runs out of tears. It takes all the energy she didn't know she had to get off the floor. She returns the book. She goes back to her room. She lies on her bed, watching the thin sliver of light from her curtains as it roams across her floor. She considers getting up to close the curtains properly. She turns over instead.

At some point, Mum enters. She sits beside Charlotte.

'You've had a long sleep,' she says softly, brushing the hair out of Charlotte's face. 'Are you feeling okay?'

Charlotte knows she should respond, but her mouth is made of cement. Even if she could open it, she's not sure her voice is there anymore.

'Charlotte?' Mum places her hand over Charlotte's forehead. She strokes her hair. 'You don't have a fever,' she mutters to herself.

'I miss Kiara,' Charlotte whispers. The fabric of the pillow, stuck to her wet face, moves with her. It's uncomfortable now. She hears Mum take a deep breath.

Mum rubs Charlotte's arm clumsily. 'That's okay. You'll be okay.' Her hands are cold. 'Just…come out when you're ready.'

She presses a quick kiss to Charlotte's head and leaves, gently closing the door on her way out. Her footfalls quieten.

Charlotte moves her head back to where it was comfortable. Now it's cold. Somehow, that's enough to stop her breathing again. So, she closes her eyes and imagines what their room used to look like.

It's okay. She'll be able to breathe soon.

'Just breathe, Ladybug. You're alright,' a mother's voice soothes. A young daughter, wrapped in her mother's arms, calms as her breaths slow to match her mother's. Her sister sits on the bed beside her, along with her father. The world becomes as small as the rise and fall of the mother's chest. Her words come from far away. 'You're alright, Ladybug. You're alright.'

Charlotte pads down the stairs. She collects the book, sits at the piano stool, and plays. Tonight, the melody sounds more desperate, as if held together by a single line of one of the staves.

Kiara appears behind her. The music stops as Charlotte runs to her, capturing her in the tightest squeeze. Kiara hugs her back, but hesitantly.

'Charlotte,' Kiara says quietly, 'we had a deal.' Charlotte hides her face in Kiara's shoulder. 'You promised me—'

'But it's not fair! I don't want to lose you—why do I have to?'

'Ladybug—'

'Charlotte Harper Wolfe.'

Mum stands in the doorway.

Charlotte breaks out of Kiara's embrace.

'Mum—'

'I *told* you not to touch that piano.' Mum's voice is low, steady.

Charlotte swallows.

'I just—'

'And you went behind my back, at *least* once.' She places her hands on Charlotte's shoulders and looks into her eyes. 'What were you thinking? This could have been dangerous!'

Charlotte shrugs her off.

'It's just a piano.'

'It's magic. That *clearly*,' she yells, gesturing to Kiara, 'you don't fully understand!'

Mum's gaze lingers on Kiara and, for a moment, the anger falters. Charlotte spots a familiar emptiness in her mother's eyes, one she hasn't seen in years. It scares her.

'I don't understand because you haven't told me,' she says, much louder than she meant to. 'It's not fair! Why are you the only one who gets to use it?'

Charlotte glares. Mum swallows, and the emptiness in her eyes disappears. Her face becomes fiercely neutral.

'You know what?' she says, voice low, as she pulls a necklace—a key—from under her shirt. 'This conversation is over.' She moves towards the piano and snatches the music book.

Charlotte realises too late what she means to do.

She runs towards the piano but cannot stop her mother from slamming down the fallboard. The bang echoes inside the piano with every pitch. Charlotte looks to the empty space where Kiara stood moments before.

'No!' she chokes. Mum locks the fallboard and walks out, taking the music book with her.

Charlotte drops to the floor. The air vanishes from the room. She holds her head as she tries to remember how to breathe, but she can only cry.

Charlotte and Kiara lay sprawled on the shop floor beside their empty dinner plates, tossing a pair of porcelain cats in the air. Charlotte squeals when they both land on their backs, feet stuck in the air—a perfect score. Kiara eyes the setting sun through the windows.

'We should put them away for now,' she says, scooping the cats up. 'I think they'd be annoyed if they woke up mid-air.' Kiara sets the figurines on a nearby shelf.

'Do you think the dolls will let us join their tea party tonight?' Charlotte asks, pushing the hair out of her face.

Kiara glances at the stairs to the apartment. 'We should have an early night tonight.'

Charlotte huffs, but still gets off the floor.

'We never get to play downstairs at night anymore.'

Kiara picks up the dinner plates.

'Yes, because you're a big girl who goes to school now. We can't have you being too tired to learn.'

Kiara holds out her free hand with a smile. Charlotte takes it.

'Fine.'

Charlotte follows Kiara up the stairs. Halfway up, Kiara stops abruptly. Mum's standing at the top of the landing.

'Mum,' Kiara says.

Mum startles as if she hadn't noticed them.

'Hello girls,' she forces, voice cracking. Her gaze washes over them like a draught. In her eyes is an unnerving emptiness that Charlotte has recently come to expect. She squeezes Kiara's hand.

'Do you think you can come and tuck us in tonight, Mum?' Kiara asks.

'Uh…' Mum's voice wavers. Charlotte notes the small key in her hands. 'I don't know. You're big girls now. You don't need me for that.'

'But—'

'I'm sorry, Kiara. I can't.'

Kiara glares at the floorboards, and Charlotte hears her mutter, 'That's not what sorry means,' before leading Charlotte up the stairs, avoided by Mum's eyes. Charlotte tries to get Mum's attention, but she's ignored too.

Charlotte gets into her pyjamas while Kiara deals with the dinner plates. When she comes back, she pulls Charlotte's quilt over her and ensures all the teddies are in their proper places.

'Nice and warm?' she asks. Charlotte nods.

A lilting melody seeps through the walls, almost too soft to hear, but too familiar to be ignored. The eerie notes, the emptiness behind Mum's eyes, and the warmth in Kiara's are too much for Charlotte's chest to carry. They push down on her lungs until all the air is squeezed out. She tries to force them away, but they're too heavy, and she's only small.

Kiara lays beside Charlotte and shuffles in close.

'You're alright. Just copy my breaths.'

Charlotte tries to time her breaths to the rise and fall of her sister's chest. Soon enough, her short, tight wheezes are replaced with deep, even breaths. Kiara stays long after Charlotte is better, weaving her fingers through her sister's short curls, whispering over and over, 'You're alright, Ladybug. You're alright.'

Eventually, Charlotte gets sick of crying. She stands up. Just because Mum wants to forget Kiara, doesn't mean Charlotte has to. There's more than one way to open a lock.

Charlotte marches to the aisle with the porcelain dolls and borrows a bobby pin from one's hair, from when she and Kiara tried to help cover up her bald patch. On her way back, she stops dead when she sees someone looking at her in the mirror. It's her, but her eyes look...emptier. She feels sick.

She keeps walking.

Charlotte reaches the piano and crouches before the keyhole. She bends the bobby pin into an 'L' shape, just like Kiara taught her, and inserts it into the keyhole, listening for the little snaps. The hole is smaller than Kiara's toy safe was, so it's a little more finicky, but eventually Charlotte can turn the pin. She lifts the fallboard and positions her hands on the keys.

She doesn't know where they go.

Mum has the music book.

Charlotte grips the chair. Could she sneak it out of Mum's room? But she's probably not asleep yet. Charlotte groans and pulls at her hair.

She thinks she remembers the first chord. She tries it. It sounds right. She tries the next one. No, that's wrong. The middle finger is supposed to be on A, not B. She tries again. That's better. Next chord. That's wrong. Charlotte plays every key within the reach of her thumb, but they're all wrong. She starts from the beginning. She gets the first chord right, but the second chord wrong again. She starts again. Still wrong.

Start again.

Again.

Again.

Her palms slam down on the keys, and that isn't right either, but they do it again and again, even after they start to hurt, harmonising with the scream stinging Charlotte's throat.

A tear lands on ivory. A mother stands in the doorway. She sits beside her daughter. The daughter forgets why she was mad and leans into her mother,

175

allowing her to put an arm around her shoulders. She takes in a shuddering breath. They stay like that for a while. When the daughter's breaths are not so shaky, the mother opens her mouth.

'I'm not sure if you remember this,' she begins, 'but when your father passed, I spent a lot of time at this piano.'

Charlotte sniffs.

'I couldn't comprehend a world without him. So, when I found a way to keep him in it...' Mum's voice trails off. Her eyes become vacant. When she speaks again, it is barely more than a whisper. 'I thought that if he wasn't really gone, I wouldn't have to move on.' She hesitates. 'But morning always came.'

Mum rests her hands on Charlotte's shoulders and looks into her eyes. 'I'm sorry that I haven't given you space to grieve Kiara,' Mum says, brushing the hair out of Charlotte's face. 'But this isn't the way to do it.'

Charlotte watches her mother lower the fallboard. But when Mum pulls out the key, Charlotte rushes to place her hand over the keyhole. Mum pauses.

'Charlotte—'

'One last time, please?' she begs her mother. 'I want to say goodbye.'

After a moment of careful thought, Mum opens the fallboard again. Charlotte places her hands on the keys. But she stops.

'Everything alright, Ladybug?'

Charlotte looks back up at her mum.

'Can you do it with me?'

And so, when all is still and quiet in Dr Wolfe's House of Whimsical Wonders, but for the ticking of the great-great-grandfather clock, mother and daughter sit at the piano together. The girl plays the left hand, and the mother, the right, until the first daughter appears behind them. They spend the night reminiscing and the dawn in a tight embrace. When the sunlight creeps through the curtains and down the floor towards the piano, they feel no fear. And when the light touches the foot of the piano, and she sees her sister vanish for good, Charlotte breathes freely.

.

Human Resources

Rachel Gurr

The Evolution of Intelligence exhibit at the museum was the only place in Neo Jericho that bots of the public could view preserved human body parts. Legally, at least.

In the Hall of Humanity, displays of plastinated human body parts and jarred wet specimens documented the many steps it took for Earth's dominant species to evolve to where it was now—completely mechanical. Every part of the human anatomy was showcased, from head to toe, male and female, young and old. The hall functioned primarily as a site for education, but for some it was a place of reflection. For Harvel, the Hall of Humanity was a space for both.

On a small bench, Harvel sat among relics from a time that preceded the robotic age. In one metal hand he fiddled with a pencil, and in the other he held a worn notebook. Its pages were home to countless drawings of hands, legs, torsos, feet, and facial features, all of which he had referenced from specimens in this very hall. He favoured physical copies of his studies. Scanning these exhibits and storing them in his memory banks would be convenient, but digital backups were too risky; they could be hacked, duplicated, corrupted…recovered. Paper was safer. Paper could be burnt.

Today, Harvel was studying the human eye. He focused his glowing blue optics on an image of an eyeball and, without tearing his attention from the exhibit, he began to sketch. Once he had finished jotting down notes alongside his drawings, he turned his attention to the real thing, displayed right beside the diagram. Preserved as a wet specimen, the single eyeball sat suspended in a cylinder of murky liquid. Red veins ran through the whites of the eye like tiny thunderbolts, and the brown iris had darkened in a way that made it almost impossible to make out where the pupil began. Robotic optics were highly advanced pieces of technology, but Harvel believed that the human eye was far more fascinating.

Time slipped away from him, and the golden light of the slowly setting sun began to gleam through the large glass windows. Harvel was jolted out of his trance when a voice sounded behind him, booming throughout the hall.

'Closing in five.'

Harvel reactively slammed his notebook shut and turned to face the security officer. He had a sleek but sturdy humanoid figure, standard among bots of the law, and his black carbon fibre frame gave him the eerie illusion of a walking shadow. Despite the officer's lack of visible optics, Harvel still felt as if the bot was looking straight through the cover of his notebook, scanning his drawings.

'Oh no. Goodness me, is it that time already? I—' Harvel hastily got to his feet and checked the time on his head-up display. 'Shoot, I'm late.' He had to get moving if he wanted to catch the six-thirty train out of town. With approximately three hours until curfew, he was already pushing it.

The security officer remained still and silent, his head tracking Harvel's movements as he scurried past, until the only thing left of the nervous bot was the clanking of his footsteps echoing throughout the empty halls.

The slums that bordered the city of Neo Jericho were uncomfortable and uninviting. They were a maze of stained concrete walls, rusted tin fences, and flickering neon lights. What remained of the daylight was shunned from the narrow alleyways, and pools of murky water from yesterday's rain still collected in the dips of the uneven pavement. The slums were a den of despondence and dejection, but for those who wished to capitalise, it was the perfect home for successful black-market dealers and underworld figures.

Harvel made his way through the bustling streets, keeping his gaze low and his business to himself. His white and red frame, though weathered by time, caused him to stand out among the rusted population. The bots in this area were shady and unpredictable, and his inability to blend in often made him a target for muggings. The contraband that he carried in his chest compartment filled him with more unease, and each step he took was driven not only by determination, but by fear.

Trying his hardest not to bump into other bots, Harvel scurried along and eventually ducked into one of the many alleyways. It was quieter away from the overwhelming crowds, but no less intimidating. If anything, the emptiness made him feel more vulnerable, more exposed. Ahead, a bot lay slumped against the wall, sitting on a soaked piece of cardboard with his head hung between his shoulders. His lanky arms were sprawled out, one either side of him, and Harvel momentarily mistook the oil can in his limp right hand to be a weapon. He continued at a consistent pace, keeping the slumped bot in his peripheral vision as he strolled by. He prepared himself for the possibility of getting jumped, but relief washed over him when he realised that the unfortunate individual had gone flat. With no battery pack in sight, it seemed like he wouldn't be powering up again any time soon.

Most of the shops that lined this alley were now empty, boasting nothing but boarded up doors and windows. The only shop that was still in business was the one tucked away at the end. A large neon sign flickered lazily above the rusted metal door, announcing to Harvel that he had finally arrived at W0LF3's Human Resources. He knocked on the door. Hard plastic rapping on thick iron.

A thin, sliding peephole opened hastily and revealed two dimly lit robotic optics, their orange tint glowing in the darkness behind the door.

'We're closed,' rumbled a gravelly voice.

'I need a hand,' Harvel said.

'Left or right?'

Harvel took a quick glance at his own hands for the answer, a shaky 'W' was marked on one. 'Right.'

The peephole slid shut as hastily as it had opened and the rattling of locks could be heard on the other side. The door creaked ajar and Harvel shuffled his way through.

W0LF3's Human Resources was a mess of peculiar items Harvel used to recognise, but he had long since erased from his memory banks to make room for more pertinent information. There were fabrics sewn in different shapes and sizes, plastic sticks with fine bristles protruding from the ends, and baskets with wheels attached to them on long legs. One shelf displayed a range of glass bottles with pastel-coloured liquids inside, and another was covered in silver utensils that Harvel almost mistook for medical instruments. To the average bot, most of it was junk, but to collectors of old human artefacts, these items were of incredible value. Harvel was indeed a collector, but not of items such as these.

'Hello, W0LF3,' Harvel began softly, looking down at the old bot. The bot's frame was constructed primarily of scrap metal, allowing him to blend safely among the rusted populace that occupied the Neo Jericho slums. However, what did make him stand out were the fabrics he wore, uncommon items among robotic folk. The long, tattered trench coat that enveloped his frame, and the frayed cowboy hat that shadowed his face, hid his identity just as much as they were a part of it.

'Ah, young Harvel. I assume you're here for—'

'I am.'

'Excellent.' W0LF3 clasped his thin hands together, intertwining his silver, needle-like fingers. 'Come.'

W0LF3 led Harvel to the back corner of the shop where a porcelain human waste receptacle sat gathering dust. He reached for the flush button and held it down for a few seconds until they heard a *click*. The waste receptacle jolted and, lifting up the tile below, it began to shift to one side, revealing the entrance to a hidden basement. The two clambered down the ladder and found themselves in a large concrete room. A messy workspace occupied one corner, and a lounging area with a few sagging couches sat in another. The back half of the space was hidden behind green, floor-to-ceiling curtains.

'Take a seat,' W0LF3 instructed, pulling forcefully on a chain by the ladder that caused the hatch to close.

Harvel sank into one of the old couches, tapping his foot as he watched W0LF3 draw back the large curtains. Behind them was a space where shelves lined the walls, and on those shelves were glass jars filled with liquid, similar to the one that held the eyeball in the museum. A variety of human body parts were stored in the jars, ranging from toes to whole feet, fingers to entire hands, lips, tongues, ears, and noses. On a separate section of the walls were a variety of human bones. Skulls, teeth, ribs, and even an entire skeleton. All of the things Harvel had already collected.

W0LF3 returned carrying a cylindrical jar covered in green fabric. He held it carefully and, with great tenderness, placed it on the coffee table before Harvel. He took a seat on the couch opposite and peeled back the cloth.

'Like I told you, genuine, and in pristine condition.'

They were more beautiful than anything Harvel had ever seen. In the jar sat a matching set of bright blue eyes suspended in clear liquid. The optic nerves were still intact and there were no signs of any visible damage. They looked as if they had been plucked from a human skull only the day before.

'Oh my, these are...these are gorgeous.' Harvel's optics glowed brighter than ever. He was completely enamoured with them. 'May I?' he asked, shuffling forward in his seat.

'Be my guest.'

Harvel took the precious glass jar in his hands and lifted it to his face, blue optics and blue eyes staring back at each other. When he looked at them it was like he was looking into the deepest reaches of space. The irises were as captivating as the cosmos, and the pupils were like black holes, drawing him in and refusing to let him go. The single eye at the museum was incredible in its own right, but these... He never thought he'd have the opportunity to actually lay optics on a genuine set of human eyeballs again, let alone a pair in such impeccable condition.

'I've had the top bots at the museum make me an

offer.' W0LF3's voice snapped Harvel out of his trance.

'They know about you? Won't they report you?' He lowered the jar and carefully placed it back on the table. The unlicensed handling of human body parts had been illegal for years. Unfortunately, obtaining a licence was impossible. Only museum curators and wealthy collectors were able to acquire one. Special branches of law enforcement were also considered. Average bots of the public, like Harvel and W0LF3, had no chance.

W0LF3 scoffed, 'Please. They wouldn't want to shut me down. I'm a valuable resource.'

'What'd they offer you?'

'Forty-thousand credits. Twenty-thousand for each eyeball.' W0LF3 relaxed back into the couch, one lanky arm leaning atop the backrest. 'I told them I'd think about it.'

'Truly? These are worth far more than that!' Harvel's jaw almost unhinged itself. 'In perfect condition, no signs of cataracts or glaucoma, the irises are vibrant and gorgeously coloured. And they're a genuine pair! They belong together! They came from the same skull! Do they know how difficult it is to find a perfect pair of eyes from the same specimen?'

W0LF3 chuckled at Harvel's passion. 'Like I said, told them I'd think about it. Knew you'd been on the lookout for these for a while now.'

'I appreciate that, W0LF3. Thank you,' Harvel said, calming from his outburst. 'These are incredible,' he whispered. 'This will complete my collection.'

'It may very well,' W0LF3 leaned forwards in his seat, 'if the price is right. They're worth at least eighty-thousand credits, but you know I'll take anything of equal value.'

Harvel opened up his chest compartment and retrieved from it his own jar. A human heart, pale but otherwise in excellent condition, was preserved in the container. It bobbed gently as he placed it next to the eyeballs. 'For your consideration.'

W0LF3's orange optics grew brighter as he took the jar and lifted it to his face. 'Oh, yes, this will do nicely.'

'I'm glad you think so. I restored this one myself, but I've been fortunate enough to find one in a healthier condition since.'

'Not from me, I see.'

'Well, it's not often you get hearts in.'

W0LF3 chuckled, slowly rotating the jar in his hands as he continued to marvel at it. 'No, it is not.' He glanced back at Harvel. 'Nice doing business with you.'

Harvel reached forward, laying his hands back on the eyeball jar. 'Likewise.' After one last gaze, he wrapped the jar in the green cloth, opened up his chest compartment, and tenderly placed it inside.

When the two returned to the ground level of the shop, W0LF3 reached into the pocket of his coat. Clasped between thin fingers, he withdrew a small tablet-like device with a cord dangling from the bottom. A soft *tap* to the screen powered it up and a blue glow illuminated W0LF3's weathered face.

'Alright, you know the drill. Open up,' W0LF3 instructed, passing the cord to Harvel.

Pressing a finger to his temple, Harvel opened a small port in the side of his head and, without hesitation, inserted the connector. The wipe was standard procedure; W0LF3 insisted on covering his tracks. If one of his customers went down, he wasn't going down with them. Despite his loyalty, Harvel knew that he wasn't the exception to the rule.

'Okay, just a moment and…gone.' W0LF3 took the cord back from Harvel, wrapped it around the device, and shoved it back into his pocket. 'The password's been deleted from your banks, but it's still with you. You're a clever bot. You'll figure it out. You have so far.'

'Thank you, W0LF3. Though I'm not sure if I'll be back. I think I have everything I need.' Harvel patted his chest compartment.

'Listen, your collecting days may be over, but if you're ever looking for work, I could use someone with your,' W0LF3's optics briefly glanced at the faded red and white logo on Harvel's chest, 'expertise.'

Harvel was taken aback. It had been a long time since someone had acknowledged him for what he was. Or at least, what he used to be. The logo, a red circle with a white cross, branded him as a MedBot. From the moment humanity decided metal was superior to flesh, Harvel had existed in a society that had no use for him anymore. It felt nice to be acknowledged after all this time.

'I appreciate that, W0LF3. Perhaps I'll keep in touch. Now, I'd better hurry home. Thank you again.'

'If you ever need a hand, you know where to find me.'

Harvel's final journey home from W0LF3's was as anxiety-inducing as his first, except this time he was against the clock. If only he hadn't lost track of time back at the museum. The nine o'clock curfew loomed and, no matter how quickly he hurried, it seemed that Harvel couldn't outrun time. He checked his head-up display obsessively, watching it creep closer and closer to nine. Around him, other bots made their way out of the drizzly rain and into their homes, but with less haste. Haste wasn't necessary if you were already in your designated residential district. And if you weren't smuggling contraband.

It had just hit nine when Harvel approached the checkpoint to his district. He watched desperately as the gate that allowed him passage to his home slowly inched shut. The checkpoint was flooded with bright white light and spotlights scanned the perimeter. Guarding the gate was a single Sentinel, almost identical in appearance to the security bot at the museum, but it patrolled back and forth on continuous tracks rather than legs. Its body rotated completely as it rolled along, vigilantly scanning the area as it went.

Harvel needed to get home. With a nervous urgency, he approached the checkpoint.

The Sentinel fixated on him immediately. 'Halt! Curfew is currently in effect. Breaching curfew is against the law and offenders will be prosecuted.'

191

'I'm terribly sorry, officer. Please, I'm just trying to return home. My train was late and—'

The Sentinel regarded him with a vacant, optic-less glare, as if he were processing Harvel's claims as they tumbled frantically from his mouth. 'Breaking curfew is considered suspicious behaviour and is a punishable offence.'

'Officer, please. I'm only a few seconds late. I just want to get home.'

'Your request is being considered. Identification is required.' The Sentinel extended a hand, palm turned upwards.

Harvel obliged, but as he offered his right hand to share his information, he almost recoiled when he spotted a 'W'. He couldn't remember what it meant, but he knew it was his way into W0LF3's. The eyes he could hide, but the marking made him feel exposed, like he was asking to be arrested. He steadied himself and continued, hovering his slightly trembling hand over the Sentinel's to transfer his ID.

'Identification received. Confirmed. Your residence is assigned to this district.'

'So, may I pass? Please?'

Processing...

'Access granted. Tardiness will not be tolerated a second time. This will be marked on your official record and may be used against you should you reoffend.'

'Of course, officer. It won't happen again. I am incredibly sorry.' Harvel withdrew his hand, clasping them together to try and control his tremor.

The gates began to rattle open and Harvel started towards them.

'Harvel.' The booming voice of the Sentinel came once more.

Harvel froze. 'Yes?'

'This is an orderly district. Remove the defacement from your hand at once.'

Harvel nodded. 'Of course.'

Finally clear of the checkpoint, Harvel scurried through the drizzly streets of his residential district. Rain had started to pour and he could hear thunder roll in over the horizon. He didn't stop until he reached home, a small rectangular building squished among a long row of identical houses.

He locked the front door behind him when he made it inside, letting out an audible sigh of relief. His home was a single large room, still lit up blue from the glow of the holographic television that he neglected to power down before he left for the museum earlier. Not much occupied the space aside from a couch in the small lounge area and his charging station in the far back corner.

Harvel unplugged a battery pack from the charging station and marched to the lounge. He threw back the rug that lay awkwardly on the floor next to the couch and uncovered the entrance to his own secret basement. He pulled up the heavy metal door and ventured downstairs.

A large, hermetically sealed lab kept some of Harvel's most prized possessions secret from the world above. The walls were lined with his drawings and blueprints of the human anatomy, and his shelves were filled with jars containing spare body parts, many of which he had purchased from W0LF3. A row of bookshelves housed copies of banned books and prohibited academic writings on various medical practices. Cutting, grasping, and retracting surgical instruments were lined with care on his workbench. A long operating table occupied the centre of the room, and against the back wall sat a large coffin-like pod.

He flicked a switch, bathing the sterile lab in harsh white light, and made his way to his workbench. He retrieved his belongings from his chest compartment, including his notebook and the glass jar that housed his precious new pair of eyeballs, and placed them on the bench with the battery pack. He opened his notebook and, one by one, carefully tore out each drawing he had sketched earlier. He then taped them up in an organised fashion on the wall above the bench. He looked at the illustrations and then looked down at the blue eyeballs floating in the jar, comparing his diagrams with the specimen. He couldn't believe how perfect they were, and he wondered just how much they had seen when they were attached to their original host. They would undeniably be the highlight of his collection.

With great excitement, Harvel turned on the spot and hurried over to the pod. He knelt down and pressed a button on its front, activating a series of *ticks* and *clicks* before the lid popped open with a *hiss*. He pushed the lid aside and gazed upon the contents, like he was viewing it again for the first time.

The pod was filled to the brim with liquid, and floating within it was a mismatched set of human body parts, all fused together to create a full, distorted version of the human form. It didn't look anywhere near as perfect as the diagrams, but Harvel had made do with the parts he had obtained, and he was proud of what he had created. With the exception of very few synthetic parts, the body was almost completely organic. Its head was disproportionate to the rest of its body, a little too large perhaps, but it had come mostly intact. Each limb was different to the next, one long, one short, one with a dark skin tone and the other with a paler shade. The torso had taken years of work to get right, and collecting enough skin to cover it was an arduous task, but it had finally been done in an almost patchwork manner. Even the hair on its head was present, dark and flowing weightlessly in the liquid. The only parts that were missing were the eyes, where empty sockets lay waiting.

Harvel reached in and lifted the body from the pod, carrying it gently in both arms to the table in the middle of the room. He laid it down on the cold surface and hooked it up to a multitude of wires and tubes. He returned to his workbench to retrieve the eyeballs, removing them meticulously from the jar. With a medical precision that was still hard-coded into him, he attached the optic nerves to thin connections that protruded from the sockets of the skull, allowing the eyes to be controlled by the brain through the wires. He then settled both eyes into their new sockets and slid the eyelids shut, and then open again, deeming them a seamless fit.

They were perfect. He recalled that humans used to claim that the eyes were the windows to the soul, and he was sure he had caught a glimpse of one when he looked at the eyes sitting in their rightful place.

Memories that Harvel thought had been long deleted were unexpectedly recovered; he had forgotten what it felt like to be regarded by the human gaze. The thought of getting used to it again excited him.

Harvel connected the battery pack to a long cord that protruded from the chest of the body. When fully charged, the battery pack could provide Harvel with a week's supply of power before he'd have to recharge again. This being the case, he hypothesised that it would be able to provide ample power to his experiment, at least for now. He hung the pack on a nearby IV pole and carried out one final check-up on the body, making sure that everything was attached correctly and securely, including the wires and tubes. When everything met his satisfaction, he powered up the battery pack.

An electrical current surged from the battery, through the cord, and into the body, causing it to jolt and jitter for a long moment. Harvel's optics shuddered, and their blue intensified as he watched his project of many long and laborious years culminate to this very moment. The electricity finally ceased to surge; the body lay still.

And the blue eyes blinked.

Acknowledgements

Over the course of our creative writing degrees, there have been many people who have helped us along the way. Without them we would never have been able to get to this point, so we would like to take a minute to thank as many of them as we can.

To Amy for her constant dedication and unwavering support. Thank you for lending us your expertise with edits and advice. And an even bigger thank you for always fighting for the Creative Writing students. Without your efforts, it is no exaggeration to say that our book wouldn't exist, even in concept.

To Lynette, for all her time spent editing, and patiently bearing with us while we stumbled through the process of publishing a book for the first time. Thank you for allowing us this incredible opportunity.

To Justina, for her help with editing, and for putting up with our endless lengthy discussions in class. Your input really helped crystallise the cores of our stories, and bring out the best in each of our writings. Your feedback was incredibly insightful, and the way you facilitated our discussions always allowed us to express our ideas without getting too-too much off track.

To Sean, for being an amazing lecturer and mentor, and for making us scared of semicolons. Your endless positivity and excitement for our work has always kept us motivated. Even when critiquing, you manage to put a positive spin on your comments, keeping us grounded and excited to keep marching forward.

To Lisa, for introducing us to workshopping at a university level. We learnt so many vital skills from our first semester together that without it we would be lesser students, writers, and editors. Thank you for your support and guidance.

To all the other lecturers we were taught by while at Flinders University, this book could not have been completed without the knowledge you provided.

To Abby, for her advice with the anthology, for her cover art, and a very special thank you for the beautiful door illustrations, which she kindly did on her own time. We're so honoured that you agreed to lend us your incredible skills.

To Harry, and the other past creative writing students, for guiding us through the process of constructing and editing the anthology. We appreciated the advice about what to do and what *not* to do. We have what countless writers dream of—a *real* book—because of your past hard work and championing.

To Flinders University, for facilitating our creativity growth for three years, and for donating us our first hundred copies. We are who we are as writers because of our experience and time here.

To our teachers and mentors, your guidance has been invaluable and inspiring. Without you, our journeys wouldn't have taken us this far. To all of our friends and family, who offered us unwavering support and never once suggested a plan B. Without you, we never would have started our journeys in the first place. We could not have done this without your support.

And to our editorial team: Jack Allen, Rachel Gurr, William Langrehr, Holly Letcher, Helena Perre, and Rose Star. We had some fun (and mind-numbing) times, but we did it.

Thank you to Jack, our 'professional hassler', who kept everyone on track. Without you, our meetings would never begin and our tangents would be endless. We're working on that gavel, we promise.

Thank you to Rachel, our 'keeper of coin'. Your job requires both financial skill, and immense patience—waiting for the bank account to go up from 'zero'. Your role will only become more significant as time goes on. We would like to thank you both for the work you've already done, and the work you will continue to do into the future.

Thank you to Will, our 'clown buddy'. Your skills with phrasing and on-the-fly editing are only matched by your ability to distract yourself—and others. Though your use of semicolons was distressing, you more than made up for it by writing the blurb.

Thank you to Holly, our 'keeper of records'. Your clear and cohesive minute-taking during our meetings was incredibly crucial. Without your dedication, we know that our notes would be unhinged and probably wouldn't include anything worthwhile or important. Additionally, your understanding of grammar and punctuation made our three long weeks of copy editing a lot easier than it would've been otherwise.

Thank you to Helena and Rose, 'speaker one' and 'speaker two', for your bravery in handling all of the communications between Amy, Lynette, and the team of authors. Between the countless messages and emails, you two handled this responsibility promptly and professionally. Thank you for being the voice of the editors.

And finally, to our fellow authors, it has been a privilege working with you throughout this process, both in and out of class. Putting your stories in our hands must have required a lot of faith. We appreciate your cooperation and willingness to work with us. Here's to all your hard work and we hope to work with you again in the future.

Author Biographies

Jack Allen

The Esoteric Charlie Hill

Jack Allen is an emerging and dyslexic writer, who spends equal amounts of his time spell checking simple words and writing. He is looking to explore various storytelling forms: theatre, audio dramas, video games, with a particular focus on prose. He primarily explores the question of 'what if?' through the genre of speculative fiction and the fantastic, with horror growing through the cracks. When not writing, Jack enjoys tabletop role-playing games.

Mikayla Fox

Matter

Mikayla Fox is an aspiring novelist from Adelaide, Australia. As of the end of 2023, she completed a Bachelor of Creative Arts in Creative Writing at Flinders University. Mikayla was originally drawn to the fantasy genre but has in recent years found a strong love for science fiction writing. Upon exploring this, she found that her true passion lies with sci-fi horror and she has chosen to pursue this as a career.

Rachel Gurr

Human Resources

Rachel Gurr is an aspiring author from the small Murraylands town of Caloote in South Australia. She has a BCA in Creative Writing and will have completed her honours degree in 2024. She was admitted into the Golden Key International Honour Society in 2023. Favouring science fiction and fantasy, she is currently intrigued by robots, artificial intelligence, and the possibilities of technology.

William Langrehr

The Gift of Happiness

William Langrehr enjoys writing in the crux of several genres: stories which blend elements of fantasy, science-fiction, and horror. Though he desires to explore writing in as many forms as he can—from video games to screenplays—for now, he is focused on writing short-form prose and poetry to enter into competitions and seek publication. William will complete his Honours degree in 2024, and hopes to continue his writing career far into the future.

Holly Letcher

Her Sister's Song

Holly Letcher is an aspiring writer with a passion for bittersweet and wholesome fiction. She studied a Bachelor of Creative Arts in Creative Writing at Flinders University. She received an ICAS Medal for her short story in the 2018 writing exam, and in 2023 was granted membership into the Golden Key International Honour Society.

Cara Migalka

How to Outdo your Parents

Cara Migalka renounced formal education at fourteen in favour of an experiential approach. Forty years later, and now teachable, she is enrolled at Flinders University learning to 'speak proper' so she can tell you all about it. Cara writes short story fiction, in the genre of realism, and non-fiction social commentary essays. Now in semi-retirement from her own business, and fully retired from parenting and grandparenting, Cara can be found most days staring out her window at the stunning greenery of the Adelaide Hills and pondering the meaning of life.

Helena Perre

Ronnie and the Amulet of Adventure

Helena Perre is an emerging author who completed her Creative Writing Honours degree as a member of the Golden Key International Honour Society. An avid fiction consumer, she seeks to emulate the vibrant worlds and characters of her favourite authors. Helena writes about people falling in love with other people, and more importantly, with themselves.

Elena Sopotsko

The Path to the Dream

Elena Sopotsko holds a Master of Journalism from St. Petersburg University. Recognised for her investigative work on religious cults, she won a competition earning her team an internship with CNN Broadcaster. Relocating to Australia, she pursued her dream of becoming a writer by studying Creative Writing at Flinders University. Elena's literary style explores magical realism, gothic, and fantasy genres. Her paintings have been displayed in the Gallery M (City of Marion, South Australia).

Rose Star

The Wolf and the Songbird

Rose Star is an aspiring author based in Adelaide. She's currently enrolled in a Bachelor of Creative Arts in Creative Writing at Flinders University, with the intention of doing Honours in 2025. She predominantly writes fantasy, though will occasionally experiment with other genres to keep things interesting. She has a love for history and spends her spare time dressing up in medieval clothing with her friends.

gp

glimmer press

Glimmer Press is based in Adelaide,
South Australia.
We are an independent publishing house.
Please visit our website to stay in touch
glimmerpress.com.au
Or follow us on Facebook and Instagram

Milton Keynes UK
Ingram Content Group UK Ltd.
UKHW020154241024
450133UK00005B/291

9 780648 463580